gather round

also by John R. Aurelio
published by Paulist Press

STORY SUNDAY
THE BEGGARS' CHRISTMAS

gather round

Christian Fairy Tales
For All Ages

John R. Aurelio

• PAULIST PRESS • *New York / Ramsey*

Library of Congress
Catalog Card Number: 81-84389

ISBN: 0-8091-2444-0

Published by Paulist Press
545 Island Road, Ramsey, N.J. 07446

Printed and bound in the
United States of America

Contents

to Corky
a good friend is
a gift from God

Foreword

It was Panic Saturday. For the first time in memory, I was free early enough in the evening to work on a fairy tale for Story Sunday and get in a good night's sleep. I sat down contentedly in my Think Chair and prayed to the Holy Spirit for quick inspiration. I then waited on the Lord. And I waited. And waited.

I was losing my preciously accumulated free time. My mind, tiring of futile concentration, began to wander about everything from finances to parish programs. Repeated efforts to return to the task at hand were met with diminishing success. At this point, everything became a distraction. Crickets were chirping much too loudly nearby. The de-humidifier noisily zoomed on and just as noisily clicked off. Uncannily, it seemed to sense and work against my moods. For the minute I felt the stirrings of creativity, it would automatically turn on and dry out the air and my brain with it. I thought of dry bones and dust. I ran my hand along the chair ledge and returned with evidence of a few weeks' neglect.

It was midnight. The grandfather clock told me and repeated it over and over the way old people do. I had lost my time, my creativity and my patience.

"Thanks a lot."

There was no answer. The crickets continued chirping and the de-humidifier turned on.

"Will these dry bones live again?"

"Oh! Is it Ezechiel you're playing now?"

"I knew an allusion to scripture would get you. You can't resist, can you?"

"My word is truth."

"And the truth is," I shot back much too quickly, "that you promised to send the Holy Spirit and he would teach us all things."

"Remind."

"Teach. Remind. What difference does it make?"

"A big one tonight."

"What are you trying to tell me?" I knew it was useless to ask even while I was saying it. It's just not his way. If he had wanted to tell me, he would have before this. But it was late and I wasn't in the mood to play Twenty Questions with myself. What did he want me to remember?

"I really haven't got time! Why do you always pick Panic Saturday?" That's not always the tone that gets me an answer. It didn't this time either. There was a prolonged silence.

"You would have been kinder to the prodigal son."

"What makes you think you're not."

It worked.

"I know how much you like that story but it hasn't got it for today. Let's face it, eating swill won't get past the PTA censors. Besides, today he'd go on welfare."

"But it has a happy ending."

"Then how about me?"

Gotcha! The ball was now in his court. The next move was his. From previous experience I knew I would have to listen closely, for the kernel of a story like a mustard seed would be forthcoming.

"It won't work."

I was shocked. Annoyed. Dismayed. He wasn't playing the game. "What won't work?"

"You can't plant a seed unless you have fertile ground."

He had been eavesdropping. Not being omniscient, I had no choice but to play the game—his rules. "And what kind of ground am I? The rocky kind?"

"You do have a hard head."

"The biblical allusion is 'stiff-necked'. And besides, my family is not from that part of Italy."

"The footpath."

That was shattering. The worst of them all. What had I done to merit that designation? The footpath where people trample the seed under foot. Where it never even begins to take root. I saw sandaled feet walking a dry path, each footfall crushing seeds and stirring wisps of dust. I was truly abject.

"Lord! Will you shake me as dust from your feet?"

The crickets became silent. The de-humidifier clicked off.

I left the house. I walked along the country road my house is located on as much to get away from the scene of the battle as to breathe the fresh night air in hopes of clearing away the cobwebs in my head. There was trouble stirring and I didn't know where or why. I walked and walked but without enlightenment. I

3

picked up stones from along the shoulder of the road and threw them into the fields. I thought of Jesus entering Jerusalem. He was saying something about the very stones shouting hosanna. Then again, somewhere in scripture it saying something about God being able to raise up children from stones.

"What's with the stones?"

"The Holy Spirit will remind you."

Something was lying deep inside me. I had either forgotten about it or deliberately put it out of my mind. Because of the anguish I was experiencing, it was obviously the latter. But what was it? And what did it have to do with stones? I no sooner said 'stones' when the Spirit reminded me.

About three weeks previous, I had had a particularly bothersome encounter with someone. I was hurt and deeply annoyed by it. Later when someone praised him, I countered by saying that he had about as much creativity as a stone.

"So that's it. So that's why I'm at this impasse."

"Thou hast said it."

"And what am I now? Pontius Pilate?"

"Didn't you try to wash your hands of the matter?"

"I was justified. He hurt me."

"What about turn the other cheek?"

"What about the truth? What I said was true. He couldn't have a creative thought if his life depended on it."

"John, you have a hard head."

"I'm not from that part of Italy."

"It seems to me you're not doing too well with the creativity tonight, are you?"

"My life doesn't depend on it."

"We'll see how you feel about it tomorrow at mass."

That gave me pause. I had forgotten about Story Sunday. I saw the faces of children sitting on the sanctuary floor gathered round me waiting for their monthly story. But there would be none. I was the footpath. God's word was being trampled by me, in me.

"You act as if you were the source of your creativity. There's a little pride there, John. If my Father wished, He could give creativity to a stone. After all, He gave it to a hard head like you. If you're going to boast, boast in the Lord. Who knows? Your so-called enemy may be using his gift more fruitfully than you're using yours. I suppose Michelangelo could say you have no more artistic ability than a speck of dust."

"He'd be right."

"Are you sure you're not from that part of Italy?"

"I'm sorry. Truly, I am."

"Then there's hope."

"Moreso than a speck of dust?"

"Just as much."

I went back home and returned to my Think Chair. It was very late when I finished composing A Speck of Dust. (Forgive me. I mean when the Lord finished dictating to me.) I was dead tired and Grandpa was too. He could only repeat himself four times before we both fell asleep.

Introduction

I had hoped to title this book A Speck of Dust, but the publishers felt that the title was too negative, too diminutive for marketability. Reluctantly (very reluctantly), I deferred to their expertise and better judgment in these matters. After all, I don't want to be a hard head.

The question then arose: how may these stories best be used? I suppose the best way to answer that is to explain how I arrived at Story Sunday (a monthly mass for children).

It was my desire to encourage children to come to church and to teach them religious truths in a palatable way, namely, through stories. Since my parents were immigrants from Sicily, fairy tales and the like were not a part of my heritage. So I started reading them for the first time when I was 30 years old. I made some interesting discoveries. First, I learned that many traditional fairy tales were rather violent if not downright nasty. The good as well as the bad were baked, barbecued or blinded. Since I am violently opposed to violence, I was forced to do some doctoring up. This was the beginning of my tampering. Next, I realized that parts of some tales were really not pertinent to the religious lesson I was trying to teach so I decided to drop them or add new ones to accomplish my objective. Eventually, under the Lord's guidance and inspiration, I started fabricating my own.

Another interesting discovery I made was that given the limited time of a Sunday homily, or a religion class, reading the story to children was not always feasible. Reading takes longer, almost eliminates body language and minimizes eye contact. I found it better to read the story, familiarize myself with it, add or subtract whatever I thought necessary, and then tell it to the children in my own words.

With that objective in mind, namely, that adults would read them and then retell them to children, I attempted to write these stories in that rather strange mode. I don't know if such a literary genre exists or if it does, if it has a name.

I hope this solves the problem of some of the stories being too long. They were not so long in the telling (most of the time). In writing one must do with words what can be more easily done with gestures and voice to create the right atmosphere. I *am* from that part of Italy. But, in response to those who asked, I have included some very short stories and some that can be read directly because beginning story tellers need such a springboard to get them started.

Finally, let it be said that if any good comes from these stories I would refer the reader to the account of Gideon in the book of Judges. When he was preparing to do battle against overwhelming odds (6:1–18), the

Lord responds to his plea for help by making sure that the odds against him become even worse. (Typical!) Instead of going off to war terribly outnumbered with 32,000 warriors, he eventually sets out with only 300. Of course, he wins the day. The message is then made clear to him. With superior numbers he just might have been tempted to think that he was responsible for the victory. However, with only 300 there could be no question but that God was responsible. The victory is the Lord's who could raise up children from the stones, knit dry bones together and give them life or give hope to a speck of dust.

"Well put, John. A bit wordy, but you're learning."

"Thank you, Lord. I try."

A speck of dust also bears allusion to the fact that we are but dust and ashes. All the great and marvelous things that have been achieved in this world, from the building of awesome skyscrapers to the invention of mind boggling micro-computers, are all the results of the efforts of man. And that man is ever but dust and ashes were it not that God breathed into that dust and gave it life, as surely as the bones of Ezechiel were promised new life with the coming of the Messiah. With our vaunted technology, the paucity of our origins is a humbling thought.

"You do remember that you've deferred to the better judgment of others?"

We struggle through monumental efforts to make an impact on the masses. Tomes have been written to inform them; endless speeches have been made to impress them; movies, plays, operas have been performed to move them; universities and schools have been built to educate them; billions of hours of television programming have been directed towards swaying them. All this incredible effort directed toward man who is no more than a speck of dust before God. And yet Jesus did not deem equality with God something to be grasped at. Instead, he emptied himself to become a speck of dust for our sake.

"I am thinking of Isaiah, Jeremiah and John the Baptist."

"I don't understand."

"Think John."

"Oh! I see. They are all prophets and if the Father willed He could raise up prophets from the very stones. Or, for that matter, from dust. That's an excellent point too, Lord."

"That's not what I meant."

"I don't understand."

"What happened to them when they spoke too much?"

"But Lord, I could go on and on."

"I know, John. I know. I also know where you're going. As difficult as it may seem, think of children *gathering round* the feet of someone telling these stories."

"But they're not meant just for children."

"I believe I could do better with stones."

"Or with dust, too, for that matter."

"You've got a hard head."

"I know, Lord. I know . . . but I'm not from that part of Italy."

The Patient Princess

Once there was a poor peasant girl named Andrea who lived in a little cottage at the edge of the forest. As it was getting on toward evening and there was a chill in the air, her mother asked her to go out and gather firewood. She told her to take along her friends Anna and Mary to give her company and to help her. She packed some food and drink for the children and sent them off.

They hurriedly gathered some twigs and laid them aside so that they could play a while before the sun set. Just before twilight they sat on a big rock to eat their snack before returning home. At that moment the strangest thing happened. A tall man dressed all in black, the color of night, fell out of the sky and landed right in front of them. The children were startled but more curious than frightened.

"Where did you come from?" one of them asked.

The strange man pointed a long, bony finger up-

ward. The children turned their heads in the direction
of his finger but there was only dark sky up there. Perhaps he was pointing to the tall mountain which stood
close by. It was a mountain so high it was impossible to
see the top of it. It went beyond the sky and at the sum-
mit there stood a magnificent castle. The children were
very familiar with the castle. On quiet evenings when
there was no stir or rustling, they would listen carefully
and hear of wonderful stories about the castle and the
people who lived there, but no one knew for sure because no one had ever been there. Many people tried to
climb the mountain, but all of them failed.

"You couldn't come from there. That's impossible. No one can get up there."

"Well, it's not impossible for a wizard."

"A wizard!" they exclaimed. "Then you really did come from there. Tell us, please tell us, what is it like in the castle?"

"I would tell you, but right now I am very hungry, and I must find something to eat."

"We have food," they shouted. "You may eat our food."

The wizard sat on the rock and ate the food the children gave him, till it was all gone.

"Tell us now, who's up there, and what is it like?"

"Patience, patience. I am thirsty now, and I must first find something to drink."

"Take ours," the children cried. He drank all their water.

"Please, now, will you tell us about the castle in the sky?"

"Yes, now I am satisfied. Now I will tell you."

The wizard told a tale of wonderful people— young, strong, and beautiful, all living in the magnificent castle. Each evening they gathered together for a splendid banquet while laughter and dancing filled the air.

"Who owns the castle?" Andrea asked.

"Why, the Royal Prince. A more handsome and noble man is not to be found anywhere in the world or out of it. Each night everyone gathers in the castle to celebrate with the Prince."

"Is the Princess beautiful, too?" asked Andrea.

The wizard laughed. "There is none yet. The Prince says he is waiting. So is the whole kingdom waiting and preparing. It will be a wedding feast such as the world has never known. But enough of this chatter. I must be going."

"How I wish I could go there with you," sighed Mary.

"Me, too," said Anna and Andrea.

"Well, now," the wizard paused. "I suppose I could grant you that wish—but I am afraid I can only do it for two of you. One wish for the food you gave me and one for the drink, but that's all. Who, then, will go with me? We must leave right away because I am late."

"Take me," Mary cried.

"Take me," pleaded Anna.

But Andrea said nothing.

"And you, little girl, don't you care to go?"

"Yes, I do, very much, but I don't think I should leave right now. My parents are waiting for the firewood. If I leave, it will be much too late for them to gather any more today, and they will have to sleep in the cold."

"Well, that is very thoughtful of you," said the wizard, "and I suppose for your kindness, I could leave you something." He reached into a bag tied to his belt.

"Put out your hand," he said.

Andrea did what the wizard asked. The wizard put in her hand a tiny seed.

"What's this?" Andrea asked.

"A seed."

"What should I do with it?"

"You could plant it if you want to."

Andrea bent down to the ground. With her little finger she dug a hole and carefully placed the seed inside. Then she covered it with dirt. When she stood up the others were all gone. Everything was still. She listened very carefully. She could hear laughter and singing coming from the castle. Only this time she could hear the voices of her friends Mary and Anna.

The sun was almost down now, so she gathered up her twigs and returned home. When she told her parents what had happened, they quickly ran out to tell all the villagers. Everyone was so happy for the two girls that they had a big celebration. The village square was filled with merriment. The happy voices of the villagers blended with the happy sounds coming from the castle in the sky.

The days passed, then weeks and months. Each evening when her chores were finished, Andrea would go over to the big rock and water the seed. Then she would sit and listen to see if she could hear the voices of her friends.

At last the seed began to grow. But it grew ever so slowly. Andrea wanted so much to join her friends. Perhaps the seed would grow to a tall tree, and then she would be able to climb up it to the castle. Each day she returned. Each day she would water the tree, then sit on the rock, and listen for the voices.

But the tree grew so slowly that months passed into years, and it was still not much taller than the other trees in the forest. Andrea waited and waited.

One day she decided that she could not wait any longer. She would climb the mountain. She packed some food and drink and began climbing the mountain. She climbed and climbed, but it seemed that the higher she got, the higher the mountain became. She climbed until she was exhausted and had no more food left. At last she realized that she would never succeed by climbing. So sadly she turned around and returned home.

More years passed and the tree had grown so high you could no longer see the top of it.

"Now," said Andrea, "I must climb the tree to the castle before I become so old that I won't have enough strength."

Early one morning she began to climb the tree. For three days she climbed the tree until she finally reached the top. But her heart almost broke when she saw that the castle was still high above her. No amount of stretching or jumping would make her reach it. She waited up there for several days hoping that the tree would grow the rest of the way, but it didn't, so she eventually climbed back down.

More years passed and Andrea had grown much older. Nevertheless, each evening she would listen to the still young voices of her two childhood friends.

One evening when Andrea had grown quite old, as she walked over to the tree, she felt that something was different. She couldn't see too well at first, but she could smell a wonderful perfume in the air. She looked around and then noticed that the tree was full of blossoms—big, beautiful blossoms—red blossoms and blue blossoms and green and gold and purple like none she had ever seen in her whole life. There were beautiful blossoms all the way up the tree, and their fragrance filled the air.

While she stood there, an old, wrinkled man walked out from behind the rock. At first Andrea was startled, but remembering to be courteous, she said, "Hello, old man."

"Hello, old woman," he answered. "I was wondering if you might have anything to eat, for I am very hungry."

Andrea looked at the poor old man and gave him the food she had brought for herself. He was so hungry that he ate everything she had.

In the meantime, Andrea went over to sit on the rock. She wanted to see the blossoms as long as she could before the sun went down. The old man came over and stood next to her. They both remained there in silence, looking at the tree, smelling the fragrance of the blossoms.

The silence was soon broken when Andrea's empty stomach began to growl from hunger.

"Are you hungry?" the old man asked.

"Yes," she replied.

"Why don't you eat, then?"

"I have no more food."

"You gave me all that you had?"

"Yes."

"Then I must repay your kindness."

When he had said that, he walked over to the tree and began picking the blossoms. He picked them until his arms were full. He then took a cup and began squeezing the blossoms until little drops of liquid filled it to the brim. Then he took the squeezed blossoms and made them into a little cake.

"Here, take and eat this," he said to her.

When she had finished, he gave her the cup and told her to drink. Andrea was thrilled. The food and drink were the most delicious things she had ever tasted. Her whole body felt wonderful and full.

At that moment, a wind began to blow. Harder and harder it blew. Leaves began to swirl and blossoms began to fall. The sound of wind and rustling leaves surrounded her. As the wind became stronger, Andrea became frightened. She was afraid she would blow away. She called to the old man to help her and he took her by the hand. With so much wind and leaves, she could see nothing anymore. Then she felt as though she was being lifted, gently lifted, higher and higher. Somehow she was not afraid any longer. She felt wonderful.

The sound of the wind began to change. It was beginning to sound like laughter. Yes, it was laughter. People were laughing all around her. She opened her eyes. She was in a great hall filled with happy people. Beautiful girls in gowns danced with handsome young men around and around to the happy music of an orchestra. Then she noticed her two friends Mary and Anna. Why, they were still young—as young as when they left her years ago. How could that be? Then Andrea looked at herself. Her own body was young and strong again, too. She was going to clap for joy when she realized that she was still holding onto the old man's hand. She turned to thank him, but he was no longer an old man. Instead he was a young and extremely handsome man.

"Quiet, everyone! Listen!" he said. The music stopped, the dancing stopped, and the people gathered around.

"I have an announcement for you. Good news. I, your Prince, this day have chosen my bride—Andrea. She has pleased me most, for she has waited patiently all these years, and she never lost hope. She had planted her love and cared for it until, at last, it has come to blossom. She will be my Princess."

So the Royal Prince married Andrea, and they lived in the castle in the sky, happily ever after.

The First Picnic

One day a boy came into the park to play. He carried with him a tiny bag filled with meats his mother had given him to snack on. While in the park he met another boy who also had a bag his mother had given him—only his was filled with tiny cakes and cookies for him to snack on. The two boys began to play together, putting their bags aside for the moment. But they played longer and harder than they expected so that when they were finished they were terribly hungry. The one boy took his bag of meats and sat by himself while the other took his cakes and cookies and sat off by himself. Well, a snack is a snack, but a hunger cries out for a meal.

"What are you eating?" asked the one.

"I have cakes and cookies," he answered. "And what do you have?" he asked stretching his head and trying to see over the distance.

"I have meats."

There was a silence while each one looked at the
other.

"When you're as hungry as I am," sighed the one,
"meats alone don't fill you up."

"Neither do cakes and cookies," complained the
other. "Besides, they're like desserts, and desserts only
really taste good after a meal."

Again there was silence while each one looked at
the other. Hunger was calling them together.

"I'll tell you what," said the one. "Why don't you
give me some of your cakes and I'll give you some of
my meats?"

"That sounds fine," said the other walking over to
him. "That will be just like a meal, and a meal is better
than a snack when you're hungry."

The two boys sat down together to eat. Standing

nearby was a little girl who had been watching the boys play. She came into the park carrying a little jug. Playing had made the boys thirsty but they had nothing to drink. One of them called over to the girl.

"Do you have something to drink in that jug?"

"I do," she answered. "But I have nothing to eat and I'm more hungry than thirsty."

"Well, we have food but we are thirsty. Why don't you bring us your jug and we will give you some of our food?"

So, the three children sat in the park sharing their food and drink together. Three children from three different families—one black, one crippled, one female. It was the first picnic. Later they would learn to eat alone again.

Simple Simon
or
Are the Stars
Out Tonight?

I

This story happened a long, long time ago in a place far, far away. As a matter of fact it was so far away it was another planet. Now this planet was almost like our planet in every way. It had mountains, rivers, valleys, flowers, people, and a sun that lit up the day, and a moon at night. The only difference was that there were no stars.

On this planet there was a peaceful village whose name, oddly enough, was Peaceful Village.

Peaceful Village was ruled by a mayor who was a very busy and important man. He spent his whole day issuing proclamations. In the mornings he would get up and proclaim: "I proclaim that the sun is up," and sure enough the sun was up. He would look out his window and see the villagers stirring about and proclaim: "I proclaim that the villagers are up," and sure enough the villagers were up. Later in the day when the people set about their daily tasks, he would proclaim: "I proclaim that the people are about their daily tasks," and sure enough the people were about their daily tasks.

The mayor was so busy making proclamations all day long that he had no time to think. This is why he had advisors, his councilmen, to tell him what to say when things weren't obvious. There were ten of them, all men, because in fairy tales women aren't liberated yet.

The villagers were just like people everywhere. They rose in the mornings, ate their meals, went off to school or work, rested and went to sleep at night—everyone, that is, except a young man named Simon. After he got up in the mornings, he would wander off into the valley picking flowers, talking to the animals, and eating whatever food nature provided for him. Simon wasn't considered to be very bright, so the villagers called him Simple Simon. It wasn't that he was dumb, mind you—he was just . . . different.

One day the councilmen advised the mayor to issue a proclamation about Simple Simon. "I proclaim . . ." he proclaimed. Then he turned to his advisors and whispered to them: "What do I proclaim?" They replied: "You proclaim that . . ." but before they could finish the mayor proclaimed: "I proclaim that." The people were confused by this proclamation and asked the mayor to explain it. He turned to his councilmen and asked them to explain to him what he meant. They told him to tell the people that Simple Simon was giving the people poor example and should not be allowed to remain in the village. "That's what I mean," he proclaimed, for that was too much for him to remember word for word.

So Simple Simon left the village to live in the countryside. He didn't mind, mind you, because he was happy wherever he was. After that confusing proclamation everything returned to normal.

One morning, after the mayor woke up, he walked to his window, opened it and proclaimed, "I proclaim that the sun is up." But on this morning the sun wasn't up. As a matter of fact, it was still night and the moon was shinning brightly. "This can't be," thought the mayor. "I get up at this time every morning and issue the same proclamation. What has happened to the sun?" He immediately sent for his councilmen. But they too were at a loss to explain this peculiar phenomenon. By this time the villagers had gathered outside the mayor's house waiting for him to issue a proclamation. "What should I tell the people?" he asked his advisors. "Tell them anything for now while we send for the village scholar." So the mayor stepped out on his balcony and proclaimed to the gathering, "I proclaim anything for now," and returned inside. The people were accustomed to the mayor making peculiar proclamations, so they remained outside, certain that there would be further statements issued.

The village scholar arrived at the mayor's house carrying his pens, pencils, crayons and so many books under both arms that he could barely walk. He sat at the mayor's table, opened his books, and began making the most serious calculations. The councilmen told the mayor, "We must not disturb him while he is at work." Forthwith the mayor hastened to his balcony and announced, "I proclaim that we must not work while he is disturbed," and returned inside.

At long last, the village scholar finished making his most serious calculations. "According to my calculations, to say nothing of computations," he told the mayor and his councilmen, "using the very latest theories of geometrics, isometrics, and calisthenics, it is an indisputable fact that the sun is not shining." Before he could continue the mayor hastened to the balcony. "I proclaim that according to the latest calculations the sun is not shining." "That was a fine proclamation," he thought. "I'll have to write it down and save it for my grandchildren."

"Furthermore," continued the scholar after the mayor returned, "it is an incontestable fact that the sun is in a state of eclipse and will remain so for at least five days."

When the mayor eventually got this message straight in his mind and was able to proclaim it intelligibly to the villagers, there was great sorrow in the land. Everyone knows that you must have sunlight to see by and work by. What were the villagers to do for five days? Besides, it was harvest time and unless the crops were picked soon, all would be wasted and there would be no food for the winter months. This was indeed tragedy enough to make everyone sad.

Everyone, that is, except Simple Simon. To him the nighttime was just as happy a time as the daytime. When he awoke and the sun wasn't shining, he never gave it a second thought. As usual he walked through the meadows picking flowers. When at last the realization came to him that the sun wasn't shining, he simply stopped what he was doing and looked up at the moon. He stood there staring at it for quite a while, for quite a long while. His eyes seemed to get brighter and brighter the longer he stared. Eventually his eyes became so bright reflecting the light of the moon that the entire countryside was lit up just as brightly as if the sun were shining.

"Hooray!" shouted the villagers who guessed that the sun had come out again. Off they hastened to their fields to gather in the crop while there was still light outside.

The councilmen were quite perturbed by this change of events. After the most excited deliberations they hurried to the mayor's house for further consultations. The mayor was asleep. It was only logical that he be asleep, since if the sun weren't shining it must still be night. So after he had made his exhausting proclamations, he immediately took to his bed. The councilmen roused the mayor and informed him of the scholar's miscalculations. "Impossible!" he proclaimed. He proceeded to his bedroom window and parted the drapes. Outside there was darkness. Simple Simon had grown tired of staring at the moon and had gone to sleep. "You must all go to bed," the mayor chided. "Staying awake at night dulls the mind." Having said that he returned to bed.

On the following day after Simple Simon awoke, he resumed his vigil staring at the moon. Once again the valley was filled with light that reflected through his eyes. The villagers returned to the fields to harvest their crop and the councilmen again hastened off to the mayor's house. The mayor was asleep.

"Come see for yourself," they cried, parting the drapes. The mayor rubbed the sleep from his eyes and glanced out the window. When he saw the light he quickly put on his bathrobe and ran to the balcony.

"I proclaim that the sun is up," he proclaimed.

"That's not the point," said his advisors who had joined him, crowding onto the balcony. "The village scholar has miscalculated."

"Impossible!" cried the mayor. "Send for the scholar."

When he arrived at the mayor's house with all the necessary tools of his trade, he sat at the table and once again began making the most serious calculations. At last, he closed his books and addressed the others. "According to my calculations, to say nothing of computations, it is a mathematical certainty that the sun is not shining."

"Impossible!" cried the councilmen. "You can see for yourself that the country is bathed in sunlight."

"Gentlemen," the scholar said, gathering his books, "it is an irreversible fact that what is shining outside cannot be the sun."

"If it is not the sun, what can it be?" asked the mayor.

"There are only two sources of light," instructed the scholar, "the sun and the moon. If it is not the sun, it must be the moon."

"Impossible!" said the mayor and the councilmen.

"We must discover the reason for this phenomenon," said the scholar, ignoring their protestations. He gathered up his books and proceeded out the doors. The others followed close behind him.

Eventually they made their way to the hill outside the village to the place where Simple Simon stood in a trance gazing at the moon.

"Impossible!" said the scholar.

"Impossible!" said the mayor.

"Impossible!" said the councilmen.

The scholar opened his books and studied them very carefully. "It is an unassailable fact that the human eye cannot reflect that much light."

The mayor had heard enough. He must make a proclamation. He had never gone so long without making one. He placed himself squarely in front of Simple Simon, shielding the light from his eyes with his hands. "I proclaim that you can't do that."

"Uh, I can't?" replied Simple Simon.

"No, you can't," the others responded in unison.

With that confirmation Simple Simon turned his gaze away from the moon and darkness returned to the valley. The mayor and his entourage returned to the village. The darkness remained for three more days just as the scholar predicted. Much of the farmers' crop was lost for want of harvesting.

II

This was to be an eventful year for Peaceful Village. As usual one morning the mayor awoke and went to his balcony to issue his first proclamation for the day. He was just about to speak when suddenly the earth began to tremble. His house began to shake and the balcony he stood on moved violently beneath him.

"I proclaim an earthquake," he said and ran out of the house as quickly as he could. Out on the street, people were running off in all directions. His ten councilmen gathered around him.

"What are we to do?" the mayor asked.

"Send for the village scholar," they replied.

When the scholar arrived carrying his usual paraphernalia, he sat down in the middle of the square, opened his books and began making his calculations. It was most bothersome to write down his figures since the street was shaking so, causing him to throw away many sheets of paper in the process. At long last he finished. "It is an absolute fact that this is an earthquake."

The mayor was about to proclaim it when his councilmen advised him that he already had.

"What are we to do?" the mayor asked.

"Have the people go to the hills away from the danger of the village," he said, gathering his books.

"Run to the hills," the mayor shouted as the steeple from the village church came crashing down before him. As he ran off he wondered if the people would obey him since he had neglected to say "I proclaim."

Even as they all gathered on the hillside outside the village the earth continued to quake violently. This fact did not deter Simple Simon from his daily ritual of gathering flowers. A huge boulder resting precariously at the top of the hill was suddenly shaken loose by the tremors. Slowly at first, it began rolling down the hillside gaining momentum as it moved along. Faster and faster it tumbled down, knocking down trees and leveling everything in its path. It was moving in a direct line toward the village. In its path was Simple Simon.

"Watch out!" the villagers cried.

It was too late. The boulder was coming down with full force toward Simon. Just as it came upon him to crush him, he reached out both his hands and stopped it.

"Amazing!" said the villagers.

"Impossible!" said the scholar.

They all proceeded to where Simple Simon stood holding the boulder without the slightest display of effort. The scholar immediately opened his books and began to calculate. The mayor and his councilmen watched in silence. Periodically, the scholar would look up from his books, walk over to Simple Simon, study him, measure his biceps and return to his calculations.

When he was finished, he said the mayor, "It is an undeniable conclusion that no human body can stop that boulder."

Such a positive conclusion obviously called for the mayor to make a proclamation. He stood carefully to the side of Simple Simon and said: "I proclaim that you can't do that."

"Uh. I can't?" said Simple Simon.

"No, you can't."

Not being one to deny authority, Simple Simon stepped aside, releasing the boulder. It proceeded down the mountain into the village, crushing several homes before it came to a stop.

III

"I proclaim it is raining," said the mayor, hurrying off the balcony. And so it was. However it was not just raining; it was as if a river had been unleashed from the heavens. It came down in heavy torrents day after day. The mountain streams became raging rivers. The dam was filled to the bursting point.

All day long, day after day, the mayor was busy making the same proclamation. Each day his council-men would go out to inspect the dam. At last they called in the scholar, who promptly asserted:

"It is unavoidable. The dam will burst."

"Gather the people on high ground," the council-men advised the mayor.

Once again the people gathered on the hillside where Simple Simon had made his home. Undeterred

by the rain, he gamboled about, picking his flowers. The dam broke loose with the rumbling sound of ominous thunder. A veritable wall of water came crushing down the hillside. In its path was Simple Simon. When he looked up and saw the river racing toward him, he took a long, deep breath and began to blow out toward it. The river stopped dead in its flight.

All the villagers gathered on a high promontory to observe the wonder.

"Incredible!" they exclaimed.

"Impossible!" said the scholar. After making his usual computations, he concluded, "There is not enough wind capacity in the human lungs to stop a raging river."

The mayor felt that he must issue a proclamation. He was about to step down from the promontory when his advisors cautioned him against it. "Make your proclamation from here," they advised.

Taking a deep breath so that he could shout loud enough for Simple Simon to hear him, he proclaimed, "I proclaim that you can't do that!" There was no response. He shouted again more loudly: "I proclaim that you can't do that!"

"Uh, I can't?" replied Simple Simon. But he had to stop blowing to speak. The moment he did the river came crashing over him. When the water had settled, the village was flooded and Simple Simon had drowned.

IV

Since the village church was still in disrepair from the earthquake and the flood, it was decided that Simple Simon's funeral would be held in the square. All the townspeople gathered for this solemn occasion. The coffin was placed in the middle of the square. At the head of the casket were the chairs where the ten councilmen were seated. On the other three sides the villagers were gathered. The mayor, dressed in full mayoral robes, stood at the head of the coffin to deliver his funeral oration. A funereal silence filled the square.

"I proclaim that Simple Simon is dead," began the mayor. It was only proper that his eulogy begin with a proclamation. "There are many things that can be said about Simple Simon. There was the time, for instance, when the sun wasn't shining . . ."

"Psst!" whispered the councilmen. The mayor leaned back for advice. "Don't mention that" they advised. "He wasn't supposed to do that."

"He didn't do that because he wasn't supposed to," the mayor continued. The villagers listened with respectful silence. "Then there was the time of the dreadful earthquake and Simple Simon . . ."

"Psst!" The mayor leaned back again. "Don't mention that. He wasn't supposed to do that either."

"And Simple Simon wasn't supposed to do that either." The mayor was becoming confused about what exactly Simple Simon did do and could do when the most startling thing happened. Simple Simon began to stir, as if waking from sleep. He sat up in his coffin.

The mayor was still busy gathering his thoughts, for he felt that he must be sure to say the proper thing on this solemn occasion. When he saw Simple Simon sit up, he told him to lie down, since he wasn't finished with his eulogy yet. Never one to deny authority, Simple Simon did as he was told. "This is all most annoying and distracting," thought the mayor.

"Now where was I? Yes, the earthquake."

"Psst!"

"No, not the earthquake, the flood."

Simple Simon sat up in the coffin again.

"Please lie down," the mayor said. "You're dead."

Simple Simon lay down again.

"My, my, this is so confusing," the mayor struggled to continue. "Now about the flood."

"Psst! Not the flood," the councilmen advised.

"I have nothing to say about the flood." He stopped to consider what he could say. Once again, Simple Simon sat up.

"Now stop that," said the mayor. "You can't do that."

"Uh! I can't?" said Simple Simon.

"No, you can't. You're dead."

"Amazing!" said the people.

"Impossible!" said the councilmen. The village scholar stepped forward carrying his books. This time he had no need to consult them.

"It is indisputable, incontestable, irreversible, unassailable and undeniable that he can't do that."

"Uh! he can't?" said the villagers.

"No, he can't!" repeated the scholar.

"Oh, my! What are we to do?" the mayor asked his advisors.

"He must be banished," they advised.

"To where?" he asked, since there was only the village, the valley and the hill that they knew of.

"As far away as possible."

The mayor cleared his throat to make the proclamation. The villagers were silenced. Simple Simon sat attentively. "I proclaim," he proclaimed, "that Simple Simon is banished."

"To where?" the villagers asked, since there was only the village, the valley and the hill that they knew of.

"To as far away as possible," the mayor said.

A dreadful silence filled the gathering. All eyes were on Simple Simon. He looked at the mayor, then at the people. He stood up in the coffin. Then the most incredible thing happened. He began to rise slowly in the air. Higher and higher he rose while everyone watched in open-mouthed amazement. It was the village scholar who shouted out, "You can't do that!" As Simple Simon faded up and out of view, the people could distinctly hear him say "Uh! I can't?"

V

Peaceful Village was never quite the same after Simple Simon left. That night the villagers noticed two little lights up in the sky not far from the moon. "It's Simple Simon," they said, "looking at the moon." They were careful not to mention this openly because they knew that he wasn't supposed to be able to do that. Gradually others began to stare at the moon, the way Simple Simon did when the sun was in its eclipse, and the moonlight began to reflect through their eyes. After the mayor consulted with the village scholar and his councilmen, he banished them too. Quite amazingly, they too rose up into the sky until they disappeared, like Simon. The following night there were more little lights in the sky.

Try as they might to stop the people who suddenly began reflecting the moonlight, lifting boulders and performing all manner of other strange and wonderful deeds, it was an absolute fact, a mathematical certainty and an undeniable conclusion that when they were banished they rose up into the sky until the heavens were filled with little white lights.

So some day, when a wise and learned village scholar asks what those little lights in the night sky are, be sure to respond, "That's Simple Simon and all his friends."

And when he tells you, "You can't believe that," you tell him: "Uh, I can't?"

The Athlete

Once there was a millionaire who sat very high up in a stadium watching a ball game. When the contest was over he called over one of the athletes to him. In his hand he held out a set of keys.

"I have a present for you," he announced. "Outside this stadium there is a brand new, fully equipped convertible waiting for you."

"For me?" questioned the startled athlete. "Are you sure you mean me? You're not making a mistake, are you?"

"No. It's no mistake. I do mean you."

"But why me? What did I do? I mean, I'm no superstar like some of the others. I'm just one guy on the team, nothing special. What did I do to deserve it?" he continued questioning disbelievingly.

"You didn't do anything to deserve it," was the startling reply. "I simply choose you to give it to. It's a gift."

"What's the catch?" One could hardly fault him for being wary.

"No catch. No gimmicks. I just decided to give it to you. It's yours free . . . for one year. Take it and do with it what you please. However at the end of the year you must return it." Having said this he handed over the keys and started walking away.

The athlete was not so amazed as to forget to be polite. "Thank you," he called out to the millionaire.

"I almost forgot," the millionaire said as he turned back to the athlete.

"I knew it. I knew there would be some string attached."

"No strings," he smiled. "Just a credit card. What good is a car without gas? It's good for all the gas you want—on me."

The athlete could not believe his luck. Either this was the most generous man in the whole world or the craziest. But whatever the answer, he wasn't about to look a gift horse in the mouth any more than necessary. He hurried out of the stadium to examine his prize.

It was a luxurious model indeed, equipped with every feature and option one could possibly imagine. It had air conditioning, radio and cassette player with stereophonic sound, reclining leather seats, a fully computerized console and a convertible top that could just about forecast the weather. He was so pleased with this incredible gift that he hurried off immediately to show all his friends and tell everyone else who would listen about his marvelous good fortune. For weeks he repeated his story. For months he reveled in the luxury of all the options.

But after a while one gets used to even the most

bizarre of novelties. The seat which reclined to eight different comfort zones became comfortably settled into one. The flashing lights of the computer console soon became just a periodic distraction. Even the neighbors had gotten used to it and had stopped taking admiring glances when it drove by.

Then one day while driving through downtown traffic the athlete saw the most stunning, sleek sports car he had ever laid his eyes on. It was a marvel to behold with its chiseled, aerodynamic design, flashy sport stripes, and doors that opened like the wings of an eagle in flight. It was indubitably beyond his ability to buy—but certainly not beyond the millionaire's. Maybe, just maybe, his luck would hold out. He telephoned his benefactor.

"Hello, sir. Yes, it's me. Good to speak to you again. I know it's been a little while since I last spoke to you. I want you to know again that I'm enjoying the car you gave me. You know, I was wondering. Yesterday, I happened to see the greatest looking little sports car I ever laid my eyes on. Now, I was just wondering . . . What's that you say? Did I happen to see all the little economy cars too? Well, yes I did. I get your drift. Thanks anyway!"

He was disappointed, of course. But all things considered he was still pretty lucky. Nonetheless the sports car would have been super to have even if just for the remainder of the year.

Several more months passed and then the air conditioning unit broke down. The athlete took the automobile to a garage to have it repaired, and he gave the credit card to the mechanic to cover the expenses.

"I'm sorry, sir. This card is no good for repairs," he called out just as his customer started to leave.

"What do you mean it's no good?" he shot back with an edge to his voice.

"I didn't say it's no good. I said it's no good for repairs. It says so right on the card."

"Let me see that," he barked, snatching the card with growing annoyance. Sure enough, printed on the bottom left were the words FOR GAS ONLY. "What the devil is this supposed to mean?" he mumbled angrily. "I'll straighten this out right away."

He stormed over to the public telephone and dialed the millionaire. "There seems to be some mistake," he said, getting to the point quickly after a perfunctory greeting, yet trying to maintain some politeness and control. "The garage will not accept your card for repairs."

"It's no mistake," the millionaire responded calmly. "The card I gave you is only good for gas."

"What good is that when something breaks down and needs to be repaired?" He was losing control of his temper. "What am I suppose to do about repairs?"

"Take care of them yourself."

"What do you mean, take care of them myself? Why should I? It's your car, isn't it. You take care of it. After all, I've got to give it back at the end of this year. Why should I put my money into it?"

"The card is only good for gas," the millionaire repeated. "Any repairs are up to you."

"Well, I won't do it," the athlete shouted into the telephone, losing all control. "It's your car and I'll be damned if I'll do anything about it. I'd rather walk." He slammed the phone down and stormed out of the garage.

And walk he did. He was a man of his word. He walked to practice. He walked to games. He walked everywhere, refusing to yield his point even and especially under hardship.

Time passed and he continued to walk instead of ride as the year crept inexorably to its close. But the walking gave his temper time to cool and his brain time to think. The foolishness of his situation began to weigh heavily on him.

"What am I doing?" he thought to himself. "Here I am walking like a fool when I could be riding . . . and in luxury. If I have enough money to repair it, I will. After all, it's to my own advantage while I have the use of it. And if I don't have enough money, I could still use it even without that luxury. While there's still time left, I should use it and take full advantage of all the millionaire has given me. With all that gas free I could take that car anywhere I want no matter what condition it's in. How stupid I've been!"

So he returned to the garage and reclaimed his prize. Then, being a man of his word, he did precisely what he said he would do. He drove that car north, south, east and west as far and as much as he wanted. The car took him to places he had always dreamed of going and beyond. And all the gas he ever needed, he got free.

At last the year came to end. In all it was a marvelous year, and the car had proven to be a magnificent gift. He returned to the stadium where the millionaire waited for him. For a long moment they just looked at each other. Then the athlete returned the car keys and said, "Thank you."

The story of *The Athlete* is the story of man and God and the gift of life. When man is formed and God breathes the Holy Spirit of life into him it is a magnificent gift freely given by God who chooses to do so. It is not for anything we have done to "deserve" it or because we are some kind of superstar.

The model is exciting, new and in most cases fully equipped. Our parents brought us around to their families, friends and anyone who would listen and showed them the latest in button noses, rounded bellies, tiny toes and squinty eyes. We were a marvel to behold, a gift beyond compare.

But after a while one gets used to even the most bizzare of novelties. Our parents stop doting, the neighbors cease marveling, and we settle comfortably into what we've got.

Then one day, most likely at school, we suddenly take notice of a more luxurious model than our own.

Someone is more beautiful, more athletic, more talented, more gifted than we are. We appeal to the millionaire. He asks us if in our looking around we've noticed other models less equipped than our own.

Later on in life the air conditioning breaks down. We have trouble breathing or our backs or legs or hearts start bothering us. We go back to God but with an edge to our voice. He tells us that we must see to the repairs ourselves, but that he will give us all the gas we want or need free. "My grace is sufficient."

We retaliate in anger. "I will not speak to you." So instead of riding we walk. We add to our burdens. When calmness and reason return, when we realize that all was a gift anyway, we decide to take full advantage of what we've got while there is still time left. And with God's grace in us, we will experience things we've hoped for and go places even beyond our dreams.

Then when five, fifty or a hundred years are over (it really makes no difference how long since every bit of it was a gift), what better can we say when we return the keys than "Thank you"?

But God's parable goes beyond ours, for his does not end there. He will say to us, "Well done, good and faithful servant. See what I have prepared for you." There standing before us will be the absolutely latest, unquestionably finest, most completely and inexhaustibly equipped model ever. "Here is Jesus Christ. He is yours to keep . . . forever!"

The Search

Once upon a time there was a great castle by the seashore. It was not like all the other castles you've heard or read about. It had many, many rooms the way all castles should, but they were not filled with furniture as you would expect. Instead all the rooms were filled with books. There were books everywhere—geography books, history books, science books, books on architecture, books on mathematics, books on politics and government, books on every subject you could imagine and some on subjects you never even thought about. There were books piled on tables and chairs, in the closets and hallways, and in some rooms they were stacked from the floor to the ceiling.

It was the castle of Count Corky who people said was the wisest man in the whole world. Indeed he was, for he had read every book in the castle. His fame and wisdom had spread far and wide over the earth. People came from everywhere to learn from this great wise man. Mighty kings and rulers came to him with their problems and he solved them all. Teachers and learned men came to him to discuss complex theories and left marveling at his wisdom. Even simple people came, for no difficulty was too great or too small for him to deal with. And when he was not busy solving the problems of the world, he read.

One day Count Corky left his books for a while to take a leisurely stroll along the seashore. He was deep in thought about matters too difficult for us to understand when he came upon the most unusual and amusing sight. There before him was a little fat boy. He had dug a hole in the sand and with a bucket in his hand was scooping water from the sea and pouring it into the hole. Again and again he filled his little bucket with water and poured it into the hole. Each time that he returned to the sea, the water in the hole would sink into the sand and disappear, leaving an empty hole once again. It was a funny sight to see the boy return patiently each time only to have the water quickly disappear— funny, that is, to anyone except Count Corky. To him it was just another problem to be solved. He wisely decided that what the boy was trying to do was impossible. He was much too busy and practical to watch this continue.

"What are you doing?" he asked the boy.

"Filling the hole," he answered without stopping.

"You can't do that," Count Corky proclaimed. "It's impossible."

"No, it's not," the boy replied, continuing his efforts.

"This is foolishness. You cannot fill that hole with water. The sand won't hold it. It will sink away and return to the ocean."

44

"If I wanted to," the boy said, "I can put the entire ocean into this hole."

"Nonsense," the count retorted, rather annoyed.

"I'll show you," said the boy. He then took his little shovel and walked to the edge of the sea. He began to dig a channel in the sand all the way to the hole. The water from the sea poured into the hole. "There! You see?" he asked. "The hole is now a part of the sea."

"Incredible!" exclaimed the count. "Incredible. How can such a young boy have such great wisdom?"

Before the count could continue, the boy interrupted him with the most amazing statement. "I'm not such a young boy. I'm over eight hundred years old."

"Impossible! That cannot be. No one lives that long."

"It's true, I tell you, and where I come from people live to be two and three thousand years old and older.

Wisdom had taught the count to think before he spoke. The boy must be telling the truth or else how could he possibly have outsmarted him. No one had ever done that—no one ever, and most especially not a child. He must know more about this boy.

"Where do you come from?" he asked.

"The Great Land," the boy said casually.

"Where is the Great Land and how do I get there?"

"Ask the book," he replied, pointing behind the count. The count turned to see where the child pointed. There, atop a rock, was a large black book. He walked over and picked it up. It was a truly peculiar book. It had only one page and that was blank. He turned back to question the boy but he was gone. He had disappeared.

"Now what?" thought the count. "Was it a dream? It couldn't be, because he was holding a real book between his hands. Was it a hoax? That couldn't be either because the child was much too wise to be a normal child. If the child was real and what he said was true, then more than anything he wanted to visit that great land. Imagine what wisdom and knowledge he could learn from those who were older than the boy. He must go there. But how? "Ask the book," the boy had said. It seemed foolish to ask a book. One reads a book; one doesn't speak to it. This entire episode was foolish to him, but it had happened. He was certain of that. There was no other recourse left to him but to ask the book. He held it before him, his hands trembling.

"Where is the Great Land and how do I get there?" Slowly he opened the cover. The page that was blank before now had writing on it. Clearly and boldly it said, YOU MUST LAUGH. "What foolishness is this?" the count said out loud to himself. "Laugh? Who has time to laugh?"

Indeed, if the truth were told it had been many, many years since Count Corky had laughed—not since he was a child. But then he had discovered books, and learning had become more important than playing and laughing. Yes, if the truth were told he didn't remember how to laugh or know what was funny anymore. But the book said that to go to the Great Land he *must* laugh. More than anything now he wanted to go there. So he wisely decided that he must once again learn how to laugh.

He left the seashore and his castle for the first time in years and set about to learn how to laugh. He remembered that his books had taught him that children often laugh, so he wandered into the nearest village in search of children. Sure enough he found children laughing and playing in the village square. He sat down quietly and watched them.

He noticed carefully that when they laughed, their eyes narrowed as if they were squinting, their cheeks puffed up and their lips curved upward. This was all very scientific to him. All of these things happened as they belched out a sound, HA! No, it was many HA's put together. The noise was HA! HA! HA!

For several hours Count Corky observed the children before he tried it himself. He went off to where no one would see him, especially the children. He squinted his eyes, crinkled his nose, curled up his lips, puffed up his cheeks and said "HA!" The noise startled him. He looked around to see if anyone had heard him. This was embarrassing, he thought, but he did it again. HA! The sound wasn't full enough. HA! He repeated over and over again until it sounded right. When it sounded right he realized that he had forgotten about his eyes and nose and lips. He must get it all together. So he practiced and practiced until at last he had all the right gestures and just the right sound. It was a perfect imitation—not real laughter but as close as you could come without being real.

The count hurried back to the seashore and picked up the book. "I can laugh now," he said seriously. "Watch. HA! HA! HA! HA!" He had learned well which was no surprise. After all he was the wisest man in the world. "Now," he said to the book, "where is the Great Land and how do I get there?"

He opened the book and on the only page it now said, YOU MUST CRY.

"Stuff and nonsense," the Count exclaimed. He said this because he did not know how to cry. It had been so long since he had last cried that he could not even remember what to do. But the thought of the wise boy and the Great Land made him willing to try.

Once again the Count ventured into the village. He certainly knew what the dictionary said about crying. The difficulty was that he had to do it. This meant that he would have to observe people very carefully again.

Count Corky was very intelligent so he was a quick learner. He saw that when people cried their eyes became narrow, squinting in the same way as when they laughed. Only now tears flowed. This was rather difficult for him to manufacture but in time with much practice he was able to do so. Having his lips curve downward, the opposite from laughing, was no problem at all. He could even get his whole body to move up and down, as happens when you have the hiccups. It was a perfect imitation. Not the real thing but as close as you could come.

He hurried back to the seashore. "I can cry now" he said holding the book before him. At once he began to sob, with many tears, like someone who was really crying.

"There! Now—where is the Great Land and how do I get there?" He opened the book. It said, YOU MUST SING.

"Enough!" he shouted. "How much more of this must I endure? Is there no end to these ridiculous requirements?" But the words on the page were quite clear. He must sing. If he wished to go the Great Land and learn of its treasures and wisdom, he must sing. He returned to the village.

He had to admit that singing was easier to learn than the other two. Singing was mathematical, with rules and scales. He could not learn the sound from books, so he went to a music teacher.

It did seem foolish to learn—Do, Re, Mi, Fa, Sol, La, Ti, Do—but once he learned the scale, he mastered it quickly. He had a perfect ear for pitch and tone. Singing however was another thing. He could sing well, almost flawlessly, but there was no real feeling in it. It was a good imitation, as close as you could come to the real thing. He hurried back to the seashore.

Holding the book before him, proud of his accomplishments, he shouted "I can laugh. HA! HA! HA! I can cry. Boo Hoo! Boo Hoo! And I can even sing. Do, Re, Mi, Fa, Sol, La, Ti, Do. Now where is the Great Land and how do I get there?" This time when he opened the book it said, "TAKE HOLD OF ME AND JUMP!" The statement startled him. At once his keen mind began to question it. Jump? Jump where? Only the ocean was before him. Could it mean that the Great Land was at the other end of the great ocean? What else could it mean? After all his efforts of learning how to laugh and cry and sing, the answer was that simple. If only the book had told him that at the beginning he could have saved a lot of time and wasted effort. But no matter. Now he knew the answer and that was what was important. The Great Land was beyond the Sea. At last he could go there. He had only to take hold of the book and jump.

This last thought brought him back to his senses. Jump? Jump where? Into the ocean? Nonsense! He would drown. The ocean was far too large to attempt to jump over. No matter. Now that he knew where it was, he would use his own intelligence to decide how to get there. The first and most obvious solution was to swim. He put the book down and hurried to his castle.

He at once read all his books on swimming and quickly taught himself how to do it. He then waded out into the sea as far as he could go and began to swim. He swam for hours, but when the sea grew turbulent, he knew that he could not make it, so he returned to shore.

He decided then that he must make a boat and sail across to the Great Land. So he read and learned and made himself a fine boat. He set sail across the ocean, but before long a violent storm arose and forced him back to shore.

There was only one other way, he thought. He must fly across. Again he read his books and then built himself an airplane. He felt confident that this time he would succeed. But the ocean was far bigger than he expected, and he had barely enough fuel to get him back safely to shore.

He was exhausted and angry. There was no way he could devise to get across the ocean to the Great Land. He picked up the book once again to make sure of its reply. It was still there, "Take hold of me and jump." He had tried everything else but what the book said. His wisdom had failed him. If he wanted to go there he must do what the book commanded.

Count Corky stood at the edge of the sea with the book clenched in his arms. Reason told him that to jump would mean that he would drown. But he also knew that he could never be satisfied again unless he learned the secret of the little boy's wisdom. He closed his eyes for fear of what was about to happen. Then he took a deep breath, held it—and jumped.

He waited to hear himself, feel himself splash into the sea, but it didn't happen. He waited but it didn't happen. He had the peculiar feeling that he was floating. He knew that it was impossible for him to float but the feeling was unmistakable. He was floating. He wanted to open his eyes but he was afraid that if he did, he might plummet down into the sea. He kept his eyes closed tightly while he continued to float.

It was a wonderful feeling, he thought—unlike anything he had ever experienced in his whole life. It was impossible and yet it was happening. No book, no scholar, no wisdom could ever explain how he could float through the air, but that's what he was doing. He held desperately to the book while he floated and floated.

At long last he felt himself come back to earth. He could feel it firmly beneath his feet again. He knew that when he opened his eyes, he would be in the Great Land. This was what he wanted and had worked for more than anything else in his whole life. He wanted to enjoy his first glimpse of it and remember it always. He slowly opened one eye, then the other. He looked ahead and then around him in utter amazement. He was standing in exactly the same spot where he had started from. He turned around again and again disbelieving. He was in the same place. He had gone nowhere. It was all for nothing.

For the first time in many years he was confused—confused and disappointed. There was no Great Land; therefore there could have been no little child. It must have been his overworked mind playing tricks on him. "Strange!" he thought. "What a strange experience!" Lost in deep contemplation he turned away from the seashore and walked back toward his castle.

The happy sounds of playing children broke into his reverie. There was a group of them chasing a butterfly down the beach. Jumping, laughing, swinging their arms wildly in pursuit of their elusive prey, the children approached the Count. At first he paid no attention. His mind was far too disciplined to allow himself to be distracted. But very strangely his concentration began to falter. He was intrigued by their antics. The more he watched them the more absorbed he became in their activity—until, at last, unable to remain aloof any longer, as if he had lost complete control of his senses, the

Count joined the children gamboling merrily after the butterfly.

Quite suddenly he began to laugh. It was a strange sound coming from him. It was different too from his learned laugh. This one seemed to come from deep down inside him. He shyly put his hand up to his mouth trying to conceal it, but it would not be suppressed. Another laugh burst forth through his lips, then another, and another. The very sound of himself laughing made him laugh all the more. He could no longer contain himself. Soon he lost all control. He doubled over in uncontrollable hysteria, hands on his knees gasping for breath. The feeling was wonderful, exhilarating.

The butterly, still pursued by the children, made an abrupt change in direction and began flying back toward the Count. The children in front turned quickly to follow after it but were bumped by those coming from behind. They fell to the sand, startled and hurt. Some of them began to cry. Count Corky saw them in distress and came over to comfort them. Then another strange thing happened. Seeing the children so hurt and so upset, and watching the tears streaming down their sad faces, he found himself moved to great compassion. Again a sense of strangeness came over him. His eyes began to fill, then overflow as real tears trickled down his cheeks—then more, and more. He was crying. For the first time in his life he was crying.

To some people I suppose it would look strange to see a grown man sitting on the sand with children and crying. But it's not so strange to children.

The Count knew that he must do something to change the situation. "What can we do?" he thought. Then, in an instant he jumped to his feet and shouted,

"I know. Let's sing." Before the children could make up their minds about if they would rather sit and cry, the Count pulled them to their feet and got them all standing in a circle holding hands. "London Bridge is falling down," he sang. "Falling down." The children automatically started circling. "Falling down." They began to move faster and faster as the nursery rhyme picked up speed. "London Bridge is falling down." Now they were all singing—singing and circling and falling happily to the ground. Count Corky was like a child among children, singing, laughing and playing as he had never done in his entire life.

Then it struck him. There in the midst of the playing children, it at last occurred to him. He jumped into air at the discovery, shouting, "I know now. I know." Running down the beach to where the book lay, he picked it up and held it before him. "Where is the Great Land?" he repeated as he had so many times before. "And how do I get there?"

He opened the book. This time he was neither anxious, nor disturbed, nor even curious. He had the expression of one who knew.

"I knew it! I knew it!" he screamed happily." I knew it!" he laughed jumping up and down. "I KNEW IT!" he shouted as he tossed the book high into the air and danced off merrily back to his castle.

The book lay open on the sand. On the page it read: "YOU ARE THERE."

Parable of the Baker

Once there was a baker. In the small village where he lived his was the only bakery that supplied bread for the daily needs of the people. Because the villagers were poor, the baker too lived frugally from day to day. But none could deny the richness of the bread he baked, for the news of it began to spread beyond the valley to other towns and villages.

One day a stranger came into his shop and purchased a few loaves. He brought them back to his village where he shared them with his friends. They were all so pleased that they prevailed upon him to return regularly to the shop and buy bread for them.

The baker's business began to prosper. But now, since he had to supply another village, it was necessary for him to work longer and harder. The stranger returned with more and more orders for bread. At last, the baker went to his neighbor who had five sons and prevailed upon him to have them come and work for him as his servants. So the bread was made and the

stranger satisfied his villagers and the five sons worked for their daily portion of bread.

But alas, upon visiting yet another village, the stranger was prevailed upon by the people there to purchase the delicious bread for them too. The baker agreed to bake even more bread in order to meet this new demand. To do this he had to impose longer hours on his servants and harangue them into working harder for him. Their complaints were met with only greater harshness and cruelty.

One day the baker complained to the stranger about the laziness of his servants. "What they need is a good beating. There is nothing like an occasional thrashing to spur the sluggard." The stranger sympathized with the baker's plight and offered that in his village the people were renowned for the whips they made. So it was that the stranger and the baker entered into agreement that the one would supply bread and the other bigger and better whips as the occasion demanded in order to keep his servants working continuously and diligently. Thus the baker prospered and the stranger satisfied his customers. But the five sons worked for just their daily ration of bread.

The baker soon was given to threatening and thrashing his servants daily, until one day, in a fit of blind rage, with a newly purchased whip, "far more effective than all the rest," he beat one of his servants to death. In retaliation his brothers turned on the baker who fled in terror from the village. Knowing no other labor but to bake bread, the four brothers took over the bakery.

The next day the stranger came in for his bread.

The Special Angels

O nce upon an eternity, God said to his son, "I love you." His son said to him, "Father, I love you too." God then said, "Our love is so wonderful. It never fails to make me feel good. It always makes me happy."

His son answered, "I feel that way too. But wouldn't it be wonderful to share it?"

"With whom?" asked God. "There's just us."

"I know. But we have so much I could almost burst with happiness."

God thought for a moment. "You're right. I will make us someone to share our love with."

"I have so much love," interrupted his son, "you'd better make it a lot of someones."

"As you say," said the Father.

Then with just one snap of his fingers God created the angels. Thousands of them. Millions of them.

Everywhere he looked there were angels.

"Wow, Dad," said his son. "That's some trick. They're wonderful . . . marvelous. But don't stop now! Keep going! I really like this."

"Well, I suppose now that we have angels, we're going to have to give them something to do."

So once again God snapped his fingers. "Let there be light," he said.

Suddenly there was light everywhere. Far and wide there was a great explosion of light. Then God called one of his highest ranking angels, an archangel, and he said to him, "Lucifer. You take care of the light."

"I will," he answered. "I'm happy to do it."

So Lucifer took with him a host of angels to be guardians of the light that God had made.

"What next?" asked the son. "We've got a lot more angels."

God then created the universe. With the mere snap of his fingers there were stars without number. Constellations, planets, comets and meteors filled the heavens. Over each new creation God set an archangel who took with him a host of angels to do the job. That's why with so many millions of things in space they never crash or collide with one another. Well, almost never. Once in a while an angel gets distracted, and when he does, things go bump and flash in the sky.

Almost all the angels were used up when God decided to create the earth. He called his Archangel Raphael to himself.

"This creation I will place in your charge."

Then God began to fill the earth with good things. He made the birds of the air and Raphael assigned angels to watch over the winged creatures. He made the fish of the sea and Raphael assigned angels to safeguard all that moves in the waters. He made the beasts of the field, an almost endless variety of them, of a million different shapes and sizes and colors.

God looked at what he had done and said, "It is good."

Thinking that God had finished his work on earth, Raphael assigned all the rest of his angels to safeguard the beasts. He too looked over all his angels, all apportioned to their special tasks, and said, "It is good."

But on the next day, God said to his son: "Let us make man."

"What's man?"

"Well, I had a special plan when I made this earth. I wanted it to be just like heaven. Since we take care of heaven I thought we could make someone just like us to take care of this place."

"What about the angels?"

"The angels are fine but they're busy watching over things. I thought this time I'd like to make someone a little more like us. Then we could give him power over the earth just as we have!"

"Do you think that's wise? I mean, what if it goes to his head?"

"We'll start him off small. We'll give him a garden and call it Paradise. We'll see how he does there. If he does well, then we can give him more."

"How will we know? I mean, you've never made anything quite like man before."

"I'll have to give him some kind of a test, I suppose. What I'll do is put one tree in his world that he can't be God over. Only I can be God over that tree. How does that sound?"

"That sounds pretty simple if you ask me. But it's

all right. I'm just excited to see what's going to happen. Let's do it. Let's make man."

So God made man. In his own image he made him. And he made him like God over all his world except for that one tree.

God stepped back and looked at what he had done. "It is very good," he said.

"That's easy for him to say," Raphael said to God's son, "but I'm fresh out of angels."

II

Adam and Eve loved their home and they loved God very much. They were very busy being God in their own world. There was so much to do. Why, there were countless animals to name (to say nothing of all the plants and rocks), there were flowers and shrubs to plant, there was food to gather, and on and on.

God was so pleased with man and how well he was doing, he told him to increase and multiply. So he did.

First they had a son Cain. Then another son Abel. Then a few daughters. Then a few more sons and then a few more daughters. Before long Paradise was filling up with children.

Poor Raphael! Since he had no more angels left to assign, he decided to watch over man himself. That was a pleasant and easy enough task when it was just Adam alone. Even when Eve came along it was no problem. But he hadn't figured on the "increase and multiply" bit. And these people certainly did.

Raphael was running himself ragged. No sooner did he rescue Cain from a tree than he had to hurry over to keep Abel from falling down a hill or Rachel from drowning in a pond or Judith from getting lost in the brush. He flew from one end of Paradise to the other all day long trying to watch over all the children and keep them out of trouble.

It seemed that every time he was getting things under control at last, Adam and Even would have more children. Finally, Raphael could handle it no longer. He threw up his wings in a shrug of helplessness and went to see God.

"What seems to be the trouble, Raphe?" God asked the angel.

"It's man, sir," he sighed.

"What about him? Isn't he a marvel? My son and I are just so pleased with him."

"If it were just him, it would be marvelous. But ever since you told him to increase, all he does is multiply. I'm afraid they're just too much for me."

"Well, for heaven's sake! Are you taking care of him all by yourself?"

"Them, sir. Yes. All by myself."

"Well, why don't you assign a couple of your angels?"

"We're all out of angels. I had no more left when you made man, so I've been looking after him ... them."

"Well, I'll make you a few more."

"Begging your pardon, Lord. I know you've been busy all over the universe, but have you been to earth lately?"

"Well no, come to think of it. I've been pretty busy elsewhere."

"If you don't mind my saying so, I'm going to need more than a few more angels. I've got kids hanging from the trees down there."

"How many do you want."

"Thousands! Millions!"

"Come now, Raphe! You're exaggerating!"

"Listen, God. At the rate man's going, I wonder if the universe is going to be large enough. Why don't you come and see for yourself?"

"I can't right now. I have some other pressing matters to attend to. I will make you a host of angels to assist you."

God was just about to snap his fingers when Raphael interrupted him.

"Special angels," he said.

"I beg your pardon," God replied. "What was that you said? Special angels?"

"Special angels," Raphael repeated.

"What do you mean 'special angels'?"

"They'd better be special if they're going to take care of people. These people you've made are not quite like anything else throughout the universe."

"I know they're special."

"That's why I need special angels."

"Tell me. In what way do they have to be special?"

"Well, for one thing these people like to play. Other angels can just stand by watching. People angels can't. They're going to be poked, pushed, dragged, jumped on, pulled and stretched. They're going to have to be pretty durable."

"I will make them *strong.*"

"I'm not finished."

"There's more?"

"I've only just begun."

"Continue."

"For another thing, these people take forever to make up their minds. First they say one thing, then they say another. They're going to do one thing, then they stop and leave it to do something else. No matter what they say or do there always seems to be more. These special angels are going to have to be patient."

"I will give them *patience.*"

"There's more!"

"Continue."

"These people seem to get into all kinds of mischief. And it's not just the little ones, although they're always a double handful. I mean, wingful. You see, they've got me so confused I don't know what I'm saying."

"I will give these special angels *endurance.*"

"That's good too, but that's not what I was getting at."

"Continue then."

"To get back to mischief. They discovered fire recently. Now all they do is go around setting things on fire. If someone doesn't keep an eye on them, Paradise will look like hell."

"The special angels will be *vigilant.*"

"And they get into all kinds of puzzlements. They're not always sure what exactly they want. They need guidance."

"The angels will be *intelligent.*"

"They get into trouble faster than you can bat an eye. I mean, a wing."

"They will be *versatile.*"

"People constantly change. They're fickle."

"The angels will be *loyal.*"

"But with all that, God, these people are gentle and kind. And best of all, they are loving."

"My special angels will *love* them. Is that it?" he said, almost exasperated.

"That's it."

"Nothing else?"

"Nothing except please make a lot of them."

God then snapped his fingers and at once there were hosts and hosts of special angels. Raphael assigned a special angel to each of the humans, from the youngest to the oldest. He put the rest of the special angels on stand-by, certain that if man kept going the way he was, they would all be used up in no time.

So it was that God created special angels to be with mankind. Each one was gifted with strength, patience, endurance, vigilance, intelligence, loyalty, versatility, and love.

Soon Paradise was filled with people and their special angels. They were always together. They played together, worked together, ate together, swam together, climbed together. They even sang together. Paradise was heavenly. Man was happy. God was happy. And Raphael was happy.

III

Then one day a terrible thing happened. While playing hide and seek with her angel, Eve ran through the woods and hid behind the one tree God had given them as a test. She had almost forgotten about it. Now that she looked at it she remembered what God had told her and Adam. They could be God over everything in their world except this tree. "I wonder why? This is a puzzlement," she thought. "I hope my angel finds me soon so I can ask him."

"Because you'll be like God." It was the snake

who spoke. Eve was not at all startled to hear the snake speak because in many of the games the children played, their angels would often hide in the animals. Then they would surprise and delight them by calling out to them from a bear or a monkey. She thought it was her angel hiding in the snake. The snake did not correct her.

"But I am already like God."

"Not entirely. You see, to be like God you must be God over everything. That means this tree too. How can you be God over everything and not this tree?"

What he said was true, Eve thought. And anyway, what was so special about this tree. It didn't look any different from the others. Even the fruit was no different. They looked something like apples. So what's the big deal?

"Try it. You'll like it," hissed the snake.

"Why not?" answered Eve as she took a bite.

No sooner had her teeth sunk into the apple than did her angel break through the brush in front of her and yell out: "I found you."

Eve looked right at him—or, rather, past him. For Eve could no longer see or hear her angel.

Later, when Adam joined Eve he was surprised to learn about what she had done.

"Why did you do it?"

"Because I wanted to be like God!"

"But we are like God."

"Not entirely."

"What do you mean?"

"Well, I thought about what the serpent said. He said that we have dominion over everything except this tree. How can we be God of our world if there's something we don't have dominion over?"

"That's confusing!"

"What's confusing about it. It makes sense, doesn't it?"

"I suppose so, but it seems to me that there's something more that we haven't thought about. Why don't we ask our angels? Mine should be here in a minute. Where's yours, Eve?"

"I don't know. I haven't seen him. What's to ask? Try it and you'll see."

"You tried it. You tell me what's it like."

"I can't explain it. It's different. It's not like anything we've ever known before."

"Do you feel like God?"

"I don't know. All I know is that there's nothing now in our world that I don't have dominion over."

"I'm confused. I feel that there's something we still haven't thought about. Something's missing."

"All that's missing is your trying the fruit of this tree. Want some?" she asked, handing him an apple.

"Why not?" Adam bit into the apple. At once his eyes were opened. Had he waited just a moment longer his angel would have told him what it was he couldn't think of. If nothing else, the taste of the fruit taught him what his angel would have said: there can only be one God. But to tell him now was too late. He was already beginning to realize it. Besides, Adam couldn't see or hear his angel anymore either.

IV

"Raphael," God called to his archangel. A few minutes later he appeared.

"Yes, Lord. Sorry for the delay but people can sure keep you busy. Besides, something strange seems to be happening in Paradise. How can I please you?"

"I'm afraid your people—my people—are going to have to leave Paradise."

"Leave Paradise!" he repeated. "Whatever for?"

"They have chosen to leave," God said sadly.

"Well, I know they're a little frisky, Lord, but I don't think they would really want to leave Paradise."

"They must leave. I have ordered it."

The full impact of what God said staggered the archangel. "No," he sighed in disbelief. "Not them too." He thought of mankind, and how much he loved them. He had watched over them since the very beginning. He had followed their growth over the years. He had delighted in their foibles and marveled at their burgeoning wisdom. He had bargained with God for special angels to be with them. What was to become of him? Where would man go when he left the garden? And what would happen to his angels?

God, of course, read Raphael's thoughts. He saw how much the archangel loved this new creation of his, how much he cherished and cared for mankind. He knew how distressing this was going to be for him. "I'm sorry, Raphe, but it has to be. Their tasting the forbidden fruit has made it inevitable."

"But, Lord," Raphael pleaded. "Where will they go. They were just beginning to learn. They were just beginning to grow in wisdom. If they leave the garden they'll be lost. They'll stray away from one another. My angels have almost too much to do as it is now. How will they manage once man leaves the garden?"

Now it was God's turn to sigh. This was not going to be easy for the angel.

"Raphe, your angels can't go with them."

Raphael was stunned. "My God, you can't mean it. They could never manage without their angels. Why, they're inseparable."

"I'm afraid that's also a consequence of their action. They already can't see or hear their angels anymore."

"Then let them be invisible to man but let them stay with man."

"I don't want to seem cruel, Raphe. It's not my decision to take your angels away from man. It was his decision to walk away from us."

Raphael used all his angelic intelligence to plead

with God for mankind: "Even if he turned away from us, we could still keep after him, watch over him, couldn't we?"

"You could, but not like before. He may no longer see you like before or hear you. He will no longer be able to walk with you or play with you. I could continue to let you watch over him like before, but in no way may you ever interfere in his life—not without my special permission."

"That will be difficult for us, Lord, but of course we will obey."

"They are leaving the garden now. I know how difficult this is for you and your angels, so I will send one of my other angels to bar and guard the gate against their return."

Slowly Raphael turned and started to leave the Lord's presence. He must do more. But what? What more could he do?

"Lord, I thank you that you have allowed my angels to continue watching over man. Must they *always* remain invisible?"

"Always, Raphael. However I may once in a while for a special reason dispense that."

"Thank you, Lord. Since they don't always have to be invisible, do they *always* have to remain silent?"

"Always, Raphael. But I can dispense with that, too, at times."

"Thank you, Lord. But since they don't *always* have to be invisible or silent, could they *at times* be able to use their power . . ."

"Raphe," God interrupted. "It seems to me we've been over this route before. Tell me—what are you getting at?"

"Well, Lord, man is a special creation. You said so

yourself. And you even gave him special angels with special powers. Remember, you made them strong, patient, enduring, vigilant, intelligent, versatile, loyal and loving."

"Raphe—God never forgets. Get to the point."

"The point is: what good is it having all those special angels with all those special qualities if they can't use them on the very people they were created for?"

"You make a good lawyer, Raphe. But you will recall that man is guilty of the crime. This is the result of his own deed and . . ."

Now it was Raphael's turn to interrupt. "And you can at times dispense with that consequence. You said so yourself."

"What are you trying to corner me into, Raphe?"

"You compliment me, Lord. You know it's impossible to corner God."

"Yes, but that won't stop you from trying. Now please get to the point."

"The point is, if you can make us sometimes visible and sometimes audible, couldn't you make some of us *all the time* that way just so that we can continue doing what you made us to do?"

Now that he said it he heaved a sigh of relief. He had not backed God into a corner; he had put him on the spot.

"Well done!" laughed God. "Well done! It is fitting tribute to your love for man. But since you have played your clever trickery on me, I shall continue the game. Your noble logic has won you what you've asked for. Man may have some special angels all the time that he can see and hear and who can do all that they were created for"—here God paused for dramatic effect—"but they must be totally disguised. By rights he should have lost them; and so they may not appear to him as angels, as they did before."

"That's no problem," shouted Raphael with joy. "I can come up with a good disguise for them."

Raphael called one of his special angels, who came and stood there between God and the archangel, somewhat bewildered over what was happening.

Raphael thought for a moment. "I have it," he said. He clapped his hands at the angel, and instantly the angel changed form. "How's that for a disguise?" he shouted triumphantly.

"Not bad," said God, looking at the changed angel. "A rather clever change. What will be his new name, since he may not be called angel?"

Raphael was feeling pretty good about how cleverly he had manipulated God into granting his request, but he felt it was only right that God should be given the credit. Therefore, if he must find a new name, what better than to reverse the name of God. And so he said: "I shall call him . . . dog."

"You are a marvel, Raphe. So be it. Man shall have his angels—I mean his dogs." With that God disappeared.

Raphael stood there pleased beyond telling. Angels would still watch over all men. Some of them would be close to him as dogs. What more could he have done? Yet somehow he felt that something wasn't quite right. What he forgot was that God knew what he would think before he even thought it.

So Raphael sent off some of his angels to earth as dogs. He would keep in close touch with them by speaking to them while they were sleeping. At such times their legs twitch and they whine as if they are having dreams. In reality they are receiving their latest instructions from Raphael the Archangel.

"Lord," Raphael cried out, "it's driving me crazy. The suspense is killing me. You said you'd continue the game. But you didn't do anything."

"Oh but I did, Raphe."

"Just because I tricked you, you're not going to be a sore loser, are you?"

"Raphe," God said benignly, "God can't lose."

"Then tell me what you did?"

"Did? Why nothing. I merely granted your wish. Man has his special angels that can be seen—I mean his dogs. And they are, let me see, strong, patient, enduring, vigilant, intelligent, agile, loyal and loving. That's everything, isn't it?"

"Not quite," said Raphael apprehensively. He remembered that God doesn't forget. "You didn't say anything about hearing them."

"Oh, didn't I? How could I have failed to mention that? Why, that's the best part. Man will be able to hear them, but, you see, I've only allowed them to say one word."

"One word?" questioned the angel. "What word?"

"Listen," smiled God. "Listen closely. You'll hear it."

At first it was indistinct, scattered here and there. Then it became louder, sharper, more demanding. Then it was clear—loud and painfully clear! From all over the earth it came up to heaven.

Raphe!
Raphe!
Raphe! Raphe!

Raphe! Raphe! Raphe! Raphe! Raphe! Raphe!
Raphe! Raphe! Raphe! Raphe! Raphe! Raphe!

"Clever indeed," laughed God, "spelling God backward to get dog. A little pride there, my angel. Oh, you really tricked me. But after all, it was your idea," he said turning away. Just before he disappeared he said over his back, "By the way, Raphe, your angels—I think they're calling you."

The King's New Tunic

O nce there was a king. He was a kind and goodly king, most beloved by all his subjects. Once on his birthday, his people presented him with a wonderful gift—a fine tunic. It was a wonderfully marvelous garment. It had many colors—bright and happy colors, gold, red, yellow, orange, and brown when it reflected the daylight, and pleasant gentle colors, blue, green, purple, silver and gray at twilight. Indeed the very colors of the garment seemed to change magically not only with the time of day but with the occasion or even the mood of the king. And it was a perfect fit—snug and close where warmth was needed and loose and flowing when movement required. What was so especially remarkable was that it was woven entirely from one single skein of yarn. It was a seamless garment.

The king so loved his new tunic that he wore it every day. He wore it for the great affairs of state and even for menial everyday tasks. It was the joy of the king and the pride of the kingdom.

One day, as the king hastened down a castle corridor, the flowing tunic caught on a rough stone which pulled a tiny bit of yarn out of place. The king stopped and examined the garment closely. There, near the bottom, on the side, he saw a snag. He reached down and drew the garment close to his face. It was a snag, all right—a small one, a tiny insignificant one, but a snag nonetheless.

The king hastened to the royal tailor for advice.

"Leave it alone!" he cautioned. "It is a trivial thing, hardly noticeable. Forget about it. No one will notice it."

No one did notice it—no one, that is, except the king. The king could not forget about it. It was there and he knew it. When he walked, he would look down to see if he could see it. It was during such diversions that he would bump into doors or trip down stairs. Whenever he sat, his hand would slowly reach down his side, as if drawn by a magnet, groping, feeling, until he found the offending loop.

When he found it he became annoyed. He then began pulling at it. Slowly but surely the loop got bigger. The snag eventually became very obvious and most apparent.

At long last, the king went to his room and with a pair of scissors cut the loop—carefully and as close to the garment as possible. It was an excellent operation. A surgeon could not have done better. The garment appeared smooth and absolutely flawless once again.

Now that the tunic was restored, the king was happy and he continued again to wear it daily. But there were times when he was bored, such as when he sat in parliament listening to some long-winded baron. At those times he would take to looking distractedly at his

tunic. It was then that he would remember the snag—
and as if suddenly lost in a child's game, he would
search the garment until he found the spot. If the light
were poor, and it usually was poor inside the castle, he
would have to pull at the cloth to see if he had actually
found the correct spot. But, alas, each time he did the
fabric loosened until the frayed ends of two pieces of
yarn hung down from the cloth. Whereas before there
had been one tiny offending loop, now there were two
imperfections to annoy him.

Again he took his scissors and cut the yarn close to
the cloth. But now there was a tiny hole. True, it was
ever so tiny a hole, and no one noticed it—no one, that

is, except the king. He would no sooner sit than his hand would reach down and search out the spot. Then, as if to mark it, he would put his finger through the hole.

Once at a state dinner, while absent-mindedly poking his finger through the hole, the wife of the French ambassador asked him to kindly pass the wine. He moved his hand to reach for it but his finger was stuck. He pulled and tugged but it did not break loose. The woman repeated her request when the king seemingly failed to comply. In a fit of exasperation the king yanked with all his might, and the wayward finger tore loose. His hand suddenly freed, released from its restraint, flew up against the table, knocking over the wine decanter and spilling the wine down the front of the dress of the French Ambassador. Only narrowly was an international incident avoided.

Obviously, the king no longer wore the tunic for special occasions of state, nor even for ordinary ones. However he still did like the tunic, and after all it was a gift from his people. He decided to wear it only at parliament where the people and their representatives would see it.

One day when a particularly troublesome matter was being debated and parliament was especially well attended, the king sat on his throne robed in his tunic. While the endless bickering raged back and forth, the king absent-mindedly gazed down at his tunic. There, once again, his eyes rested on the offending flaw. It was no longer a trivial snag or a group of insignificant frayed ends. Now it was a hole—a full-fledged, highly visible, most noticeable, God-awful hole.

Perhaps it was the heat of the day; or perhaps it was because he did not listen to the tailor who cautioned him; or perhaps it was the embarrassing memory of the incident with the ambassador's wife; or perhaps it was his annoyance at this interminable debate.

Whatever it was, the king reached down in anger and took hold of a frayed thread of yarn and began pulling away furiously. He pulled and pulled. Gradually the cloth began to unravel.

At first, as he sat there pulling away at the yarn, no one noticed, for the debate still held everyone's attention. However, the more the king tugged away and the more the cloth unraveled, the more infuriated he became. Eventually, the king's activity became noticed. The spectators poked one another and pointed to the throne.

The king continued. The tunic unraveled more and more. There was a growing silence in the hall as all attention turned to the king. Now even the debaters ceased their harangue and turned toward the throne.

The king was oblivious of all time and place. He was caught up in a frenzy. There was no longer rhyme or reason—only purpose. He stood up in full view of the assembly pulling away madly at the yarn. At times his hands caught and struggled in a yarn-web of his own making. Then he would pull it loose, casting the bundled yarn aside, only to continue unraveling. Steadily the tunic began to vanish. The hem rose higher and higher and higher until in one last spurt of frantic energy the king tore the remaining last threads of the tunic from his body. He stood there, in front of his throne before the assembled throng of parliament, panting, and naked.

At first there was a profound, awesome, shocking silence. Then from the crowd someone began to laugh. Then another. And another. And another. The king looked so silly standing there naked with the unraveled tunic at his feet, that eventually even the most reserved and sedate of the parliamentarians began to laugh. Laughter filled the grand hall and echoed loudly throughout the castle corridors. The barons laughed; the lords laughed; the nobles laughed; the envoys laughed; the peasants laughed. Everyone laughed—everyone except the king.

The king, realizing what he had done, looked around slowly at the price of his folly. "I am king," he thought, "and a king should not be foolish. My people are laughing at me." The king began to cry.

When the lords and nobles saw the king cry, they ceased their merriment. It was unseemly to laugh at his misfortune, so they fell silent.

The peasants also stopped their laughter, for it was wrong to laugh at the king's shame.

The entire assembled throng became silent. There was not a sound, not a murmer as all eyes gazed at the bowed figure of the naked king.

It is recorded in the annals of that kingdom: "Parliament did no further business that day."

A Speck of Dust

Once upon a time there was a speck of dust. He lived in a house high up on a ledge near the ceiling. At first he lived there alone. While life there was pleasant it was rather lonely. Each day he would peer out over the ledge and watch the activity that went on in the living room below. Most of all he loved to watch young Mary who came into the room every afternoon to play. She so filled the loneliness of his days that life only had meaning and joy to him when she was present. He fell deeply in love with her.

In time another speck of dust came to share the ledge with him. It was wonderful to have company, to have someone to talk to, to pour out his heart to.

"I'm in love," said Speck to his new companion without even so much as an introduction.

The other, looking around and seeing no one else, was puzzled and asked: "With whom?"

Speck leaned over the ledge and pointed down.

Other looked down and gasped. "With her? Ugh," he shuttered. "She's . . . she's human."

"I know," said Speck, "but I love her anyway."

"What good is it? Humans won't have anything to do with us!"

"She's different," protested Speck. "I've been watching her. She's gentle and kind."

"What good is that to you? She doesn't even know you exist."

Other was right and Speck knew it. But his heart spoke more strongly than his head. His love had been challenged and now his pride would not bear it.

"She will," he trembled, "and I'm going down there to tell her."

"You're going to do what?" gasped Other. "Are you crazy?"

"Yes, I'm going to tell her. Life without her is nothing," he continued, speaking out loud to himself, his courage growing with each statement. "I must tell her. It is the one purpose of my life. Nothing else matters."

Other could only shake his head in disbelief. He knew well the ways of dust. Once they had set out their course, rightly or wrongly, there would be no change, no appeal. It must be.

Speck gazed down at Mary seated far below him on the living room rug. He trembled at the prospect of what he was about to do. "I will float down to her cheek," he said. He spoke to keep up his courage, to assure that his decision would be unalterable. "If I could just touch her cheek, that touch alone will tell her that she is beautiful and kind and that I love her." Then there was silence—a silence that spoke loudly of fear, of

hesitation, of uncertainty. But the die was cast. He must make his move. He did. He jumped.

Slowly—ever so slowly—he floated toward his destiny. She was below him, and he drew nearer and nearer. When he was just above her head he altered his descent ever so slightly, so as to land on her cheek. He was almost there.

At the last possible moment Mary's attention was diverted and she turned her head. Instead of landing on her cheek, Speck came to rest on the tip of her nose.

"Ah! Ah! Ah! Chooo!" she exploded. Speck was sent tumbling violently across the room. He came to a smashing halt against a window and fell to the sill. The sudden turn of events left him stunned. All was lost. His great moment had come and gone. As he lay there dejectedly on the sill, Mary came walking toward him. All was not lost! Destiny, while fickle, was kind. He would try again.

In a trice Mary went to the window and opened it. At precisely that moment Speck was preparing to leap in his second attempt to reach her. A strong breeze blew across the sill, and in spite of his desperate effort, he was caught in mid-leap and blown out of the house. He could do nothing. His puny strength was lost in the power of the wind. He was carried up and blown farther and farther away from his heart's one great desire. Fate was cruel. Was what he wanted so much? He continued to float upward, to the higher regions of the atmosphere. Mary's house and the village itself were less than a speck of dust below him.

The air here was extremely cold. Speck began to feel a change taking place. He noticed that there was a fine layer of white frost enveloping him. It looked like a cottony winter coat. He floated by himself for a while. At first he felt dejected, then just blank. Finally he noticed another frost-covered speck floating nearby.

The other called out to him: "Hey! Come on over. Keep me company." His voice quivered from the cold.

"Why not?" thought Speck. "If we stick together I might get warm." He floated over to the other and they huddled together. Soon they saw other specks of dust nearby and called out to them to join them. The others came in increasing numbers until they grew and grew into a large billowy cloud.

Smaller clouds nearby called out: "Can we join you?"

"Sure," they replied. "The more we are, the warmer we'll get."

The cloud got bigger and bigger. As they expected, they also got warmer. "It's pleasant to have so many people to talk to," Speck thought. It also helped to get his mind off his anguish. All the specks of dust chattered away quite happily. Their joy was like a magnet drawing others into the gaggle.

However, it wasn't long before they began to feel too crowded. The pressure of so many pressed so hard against one another eventually set them to complaining. Still the cloud grew and got heavier. As it got heavier it began to drop. The change in movement upset everyone. They began grumbling quite loudly.

Far below in the village the sound of thunder sent the people scurrying into their homes. The grumbling became louder, more violent. The pressure became too intense. There was a crying need for release. Feeling the need for independence, Speck and the others abandoned their community and scattered each to his own destiny.

"Hey, look at me," thought Speck. "I've changed. Why . . . why . . . I'm a raindrop." The feeling was wonderful, different, liberating. "Wheeeee!" he shouted as he dropped steadily back to earth.

He landed with a violent splash in a puddle of water. The jolt rattled him. But before he could assess his new situation he began to sink into the cold dark earth.

"What now?" he thought. "Is this where it's to end?"

Once inside the earth he could see nothing—but he could hear. What he heard was a peculiar sound. It was a slurping sound: the sound of liquid being sucked in like someone drinking through a straw. It came from the roots of plants drinking the water that had penetrated the soil. Just as he realized what was happening, Speck was sucked in by one of the roots.

As more water was being taken in behind him, Speck began moving upward quite rapidly until at last he reached the top and could go no further. Once again a peculiar feeling came over him. It was a pleasant feeling but very strange. Somehow he knew he was being changed again, that he was no longer a drop of water.

It was night now. So much had happened to him that he didn't have time to put it all together. But he was much too tired to think deeply, so he fell asleep, wondering what the morning would reveal.

The early morning sun warmed the earth to life. The birds began chattering about what they would have for breakfast while the busy bees hummed to themselves as they moved from flower to flower. Even with all this the exhausted Speck would not have awakened had not a bee walked across his face and startled him.

"My goodness," he said to himself. "What's happened to me?" He stretched himself as much as he could so that he could take a good look at himself. "Oh, my! Look at me now. I'm a flower."

Indeed, Speck had become a flower. It was a whole new experience for him and the change was exciting.

His new life had begun in a garden. All about him there were beautiful flowers; roses, violets, petunias, and many others, all different, all beautiful. He was still gazing about the garden when he saw the house. Could it be? He looked carefully, straining. It was! It was! It was Mary's house. As he let out a cry of joy he saw her come running out of the house toward the garden. His heart began to beat wildly. The water surged in his veins. Every part of his leafy body trembled. She was coming closer now, picking flowers on her way, holding them to her face, sniffing them, pressing them to her cheek.

The old desire, almost forgotten, was reborn in him. He would at last have his dream come true—not as a speck of dust, nor as a raindrop but as a flower. He waited breathlessly as Mary stooped over to him.

Her hand stopped in mid-flight. She reached beyond Speck and picked a rose growing behind him. Then she continued on her way and ran back into the house.

"Mary, you forgot me," he shouted. "Pick me. Pick me too."

The door of the house closed behind her. It was as if the world had closed him out. "Mary, come out! Please come out and pick me." His head drooped with overwhelming sadness.

"Don't be silly."

The voice startled Speck. He looked to see who was speaking to him. It was the snapdragon.

"Pick you indeed. Whatever for?" she chided.

"Why not?" pouted Speck. "Why shouldn't she pick me?"

"Because you're a dandelion, that's why," she retorted huffily. "Humans don't pick dandelions."

Speck was confused. This was all so new to him. What did she mean?

"Why don't they pick dandelions?" he asked.

"Because you're a weed." Her words cut into his dreams.

"What do they do with us?" He was almost too afraid to ask.

"They pull you out by the roots and throw you away. That's what they do to weeds."

Once again fate had proven itself to be cruel. To have gone through so much only to discover that it was all for nothing! He could not bear it, but he would not show it, especially to the snapdragon. He tried hard to straighten his drooping head. "She'll pick me. You just wait and see."

But she didn't pick him. As a matter of fact Mary didn't pick any flowers at all. Day followed after day but she did not come outdoors again. Speck lost all hope.

Time didn't seem to matter anymore. One day, five days, ten days—what difference did it make? Mary had not returned to the garden for an eternity. But someone else did. She was singing to herself quite happily as she made her way steadily toward Speck. Before he knew what was happening her quick knife had severed him from the earth he was attached to but no longer a part of. She placed him in the sack she was carrying and closed out the last remnants of sunlight, hope and life. No matter. Without Mary there was no life for Speck. He fell asleep.

How long he had been asleep he couldn't say. When he awoke he was aware that another change had taken place. Once again he felt strangely different.

He struggled to remember what happened to him after he was taken from the garden but he couldn't. Then he heard voices. He strained to listen.

"Yes, Mary is still sick. She has been sick for some days now."

"I've brought something for her. I'm sure it will help to make her well again."

"What is it?"

"It's something my family has used for generations."

"Well, if you think it will help."

Mary's mother removed the bottle of dandelion wine from the bag. The first thing Speck saw was Mary. He could not believe his eyes. He wanted to shout and scream for joy. Would he get to touch her at last? After so long a journey was it finally to happen? All he could say was "Mary, Mary, Mary," over and over again as the glass was lifted to her pale lips.

Speck breathed a long, joyful sigh of relief: "Not to her cheek but to her lips. I will end with a kiss."

Incredible! It wasn't over. He was changing again. He knew it. He felt it. "Whatever happens now makes no difference," he thought. "I accomplished my heart's one great desire. It turned out even better than I had hoped for. I didn't just touch her cheek. I kissed her lips. It is enough. I am finished.

The strange transformation was almost over. The realization of what was happening came to him slowly. When it was completed he felt overwhelmed. This was beyond all expectation—beyond imagination. But it was wonderful. It was magnificent. It was incredible. He had become . . . Mary!

It's a Strange World

"Well, school's over now," the teacher said to the child, "and summer's here. You've graduated from kindergarten and now you must go out and learn from it."

"What am I supposed to do?"

"Keep your eyes open and observe."

So off went the child into the world with his eyes wide open. He looked and looked and was amazed at the strangeness of the world he lived in. People were the most interesting of all. Now that he was being observant, he noticed things he never did before. He saw all kinds of people—square people; big round people; tall, skinny people; red people, blue people, purple people, even green people. Some people were really interesting. There were those who constantly changed size and shape and color; some could fade in and out. He was confused by people who would point to themselves and cry and people who would point to others and laugh.

When he had seen his fill, he went back to the teacher and told him everything he had seen. "Why?" he asked.

"It's a strange world," the teacher said. "Go back and this time notice what they are doing."

So he did. He noticed that the big, round people ate Cheerios and hamburgers; the skinny people ate string beans and spaghetti; the square people ate Wheat Chex and waffles. "This is funny," he thought as he watched the blue people eat blueberries, the red people eat strawberries, the purple people eat grapes, and the green people eat vegetables.

He went back and told all this to his teacher.

"What about the others?" the teacher asked. The child said, "I noticed that the people who kept disappearing ate nothing but ice cubes. When I watched those who kept changing, they kept eating different things. But the oddest of all were the people who pointed to themselves and cried, and pointed to others and laughed. "What did they eat?" asked the teacher. "Alphabet soup," he answered. "But the ones who pointed to themselves only ate the 'I's' and those who pointed to the others only ate the 'U's."

The teacher sat back and smiled. "Well, what did you learn about the world this summer?"

"I learned that people are what they eat. Is that always so?"

"That's always so," replied the teacher.

"It's a strange world," thought the child.

The Captive Princess
or
Whatever Happened to the Magic Wand?

I

Once upon a certain time there were two kingdoms—the Kingdom of the East and the Kingdom of the West. The kingdoms were very
much alike and I suppose not too unlike the kingdoms
of today. They both had rich people and poor people,
tall people and short people, even fat people and skinny
people. Everything was just the way it is today, except
that in the two kingdoms there were no sick people.

The two kingdoms were divded by the Shallow
River. In the center of this river, between the two kingdoms, there was a large ominous island. The island was
surrounded by dense thickets and what was called the
Impenetrable Forest. This was the domain of the dread-

ful dragon. It was said that anyone who set foot on this island was immediately whisked away by the demon and taken to the center of the island where a horrible fate awaited him. It was for this reason that everyone referred to the island as the Land of Yucch.

As I said before, "once upon a certain time," there was great excitement in the Kingdom of the East. The beautiful Princess Purity was to be wed to the handsome Prince Gallant, heir apparent to the Kingdom of the West. With all the betrothal arrangements already made, the princess and her entourage set out for the prince's castle where according to custom the nuptials were to take place.

After a journey of several days, the travelers came to rest at the Shallow River at a point opposite the Land of Yucch. The Royal Advisor to the princess approached Her Highness with a suggestion.

"Your Grace, our journey has progressed far more slowly than we had planned. (He was careful not to mention that it was all because of the added excess baggage she had decided to bring along.) I fear that we may be further delayed as we journey around the island."

It was the custom in those days to avoid the island like the plague. Visitors traveling west to east or vice versa traveled as far north or south as necessary in order to avoid crossing the island. This of course was a great inconvenience, but no one was so foolish as to try to cut across the Land of Yucch. Fireside tales recounted at late night hours warned of the dangers and the folly of such a course.

"What is it you suggest?" asked the princess.

"That we cut across the island." He was careful not to refer to it by name.

"But what of the dangers? What of the dreadful dragon?" cried the princess.

"Nonsense and foolish tales," he retorted quickly.

Now every good advisor knows that he must talk convincingly and quickly in order to sway his listeners. It was not without reason that he was chosen as the royal advisor to both kingdoms. He could outtalk, whether he knew what he was talking about or not, and outconvince, whether he knew any facts or not, any one hundred people in both kingdoms. He had promised the envoy of Prince Gallant that the princess, whose reputation for tardiness long preceded her, would arrive on time for the wedding. His honor and his word were at stake.

"But . . ." began the princess.

"Only fools make up tales," he interrupted quickly. He straightened himself to full stature, held his head high, and took a deep breath, puffing up his chest which gave him the appearance of a toy wooden soldier—a general of course. With so much air in his lungs he could talk continuously for almost five minutes without taking a breath. "These are the ridiculous stories of old wives and ignorant peasants who use them to frighten their children so as to keep them from wandering off and getting lost and upsetting the family who would then have to go off looking for them which would mean that husbands would have to leave their manly chores and wives their household tasks, gather together all their children to make sure that the other ones remain safe at home while the elders are out searching for the lost child, which would seriously inconvenience the whole household to say nothing of the villagers because if one child were to be permitted to get lost with impunity, heaven knows what encouragement that would be to other children who need very little incentive indeed to follow in the wayward ways of others, occasioning a wholesale exodus of impressionable children followed after anxiously by distraught parents and annoyed relatives, for surely all commerce would then cease until the wandering vagabonds would be returned home once more. This is why such tales are invented."

"But ..." exhorted the princess, seemingly not convinced. Old fears are not easily forgotten or put aside.

"Tales of a dreadful dragon are no less foolish," he continued dauntlessly when he saw that he had not won his point. Her "but" gave him time for a quick breath, although if he had to, he could have continued on without it. "Dragons are a concoction of ignorance that appeal to people of simple minds because they have not taken the time or effort to educate themselves in the advanced sciences and technologies of our times which clearly illuminate all previously dark and unenlightened corners of our minds and shed new understanding on ancient fears that cropped up because the unexplainable was always in the power of hands that were not human and therefore far more powerful than what man was capable of doing or understanding necessitating some corporeal form in order to minimize its awesomeness and the fear of its otherwise universal pervasiveness but appropriately overwhelming so as to maintain its irrational integrity and still maintain its inevitable ability to frighten uneducated people with simple minds. This is why we have dragons."

The princess yielded, either because she did not want to appear to be an old wife telling tales, or because she did not want to be considered an uneducated peasant with a simple mind, or because her advisor had

spoken so quickly she didn't have time to think, or because he spoke so intelligently and she didn't understand him, or because she was certain that if she didn't give in he would never shut up and they would really be late for the wedding.

Fortunately (or unfortunately) there just happened to be a boat moored at the riverside. I suppose it's because it always seems easier to get into trouble than out of it. This would have been good advice for the Royal Advisor.

In order to show the others that there was nothing to be afraid of, the Royal Advisor and Princess Purity set out first. The moment they set foot on the other side of the river, the breathless quiet was shattered by a hideous cry. Out of the sky, swooping down on the unsuspecting pair, was the old wives' tale.

"It's every man for himself," shouted the Royal

Advisor who quickly ran back to the river, leaving the princess alone to figure out her fate. She was thinking to herself. "That's foolish advice since I'm not a man," when the dragon seized her in its claws and flew off with her up over the dense thickets and the impenetrable forest, deep into the Land of Yucch.

II

When the news reached Prince Gallant about the fate of his bride-to-be, he resolved without hesitation to rescue her. However he was not certain how he should do this. He would have gone to the Royal Advisor as was the custom, but understandably he was nowhere to be found. In his absence Prince Gallant therefore decided to call upon the Wonderful Wizard.

Not since he had been a child had the prince set foot in the wizard's castle. Nor could he remember ever seeing the wonderful man busy at his work. For busy he was indeed. The room where he found him was filled floor to ceiling with machines—machines that blinked and buzzed and whirred while the wizard moved hither and yon at a frantic pace pressing buttons, pulling levers and turning wheels.

"What can I do for you?" asked the wizard.

"Help me to rescue Princess Purity," the prince stammered, unaccountably afraid. Before he could explain to the wizard the details of the princess' misfortune, the prince was informed by the marvelous man that he was totally familiar with the situation.

"Then you will help me. You will come with me," shouted the exuberant youth.

"I will help you," replied the wizard, "but I cannot come with you. As you can see, I have so much to do here that I cannot leave. But don't worry. I will give you something to take with you." The wizard swung an arm up into the air, reaching out with his hand as if to grasp something. Suddenly there was the sound of thunder, and a howling wind blew through the room. When he brought his hand down again it held what appeared to be a small bolt of lightning.

The prince looked puzzled, afraid to take it, although it was held out to him.

"It's a magic wand," the wizard said reassuringly. "Take it. It will not harm you. It will help you. It has great power."

With a trembling hand the prince cautiously took the wand. It felt harmless enough. The thought surfaced the question, "How am I to use it?"

"When the time comes you will know," replied the wizard. He turned back to his machines and levers without another word. The interview was over.

III

Prince Gallant approached the Shallow River with indecision. It was not that he was lacking in courage, for he had faced many a formidable foe with unwavering valor. It was facing the unknown that made him hesitate. He could stand eye-to-eye against a hundred dragons, but the prospect of what he would find deep within the forbidden land gave slight pause to his progress across the river.

No sooner had he set foot on Yucch soil than the awful, ungodly screech of the dragon rent the still air. In one quick motion the prince drew his magic wand as if it were a sword. He raised it above his head to meet the onslaught of the descending dragon when a strange thing began to happen. From the point of the wand, a heavy white smoke began to spew forth, and so thickly that within moments Prince Gallant and the surrounding area were invisibly shielded from the demon's claws by a protective cloud of smoke. The monster rose above the cloud, his head searching, moving back and forth, confused by the sudden phenomenon. Yet his eyes were quick and alert to discover where the prince might be. Still hovering, the dragon lowered its legs into the smoke, its claws grasping in a vain attempt to capture its prey. Repeated attempts still availed nothing.

When, at last, almost the entire beach was covered with smoke, the dreadful dragon roared a frightful bellow of anger and frustration and flew away.

Not so foolish as to wait for the air to clear and allow the dragon to return, the prince made his way slowly to the Impenetrable Forest. There were so many trees, so thickly covering the land, that he knew at once that it was hopeless to proceed. Their gnarled and twisted trunks were like a solid wall hindering his passage. The branches overhead so interlocked with one another, forming a tight weave of leaves, that they completely blocked out all light from the sun. Even if he were able to wind his way through the trees, a most unlikely possibility, it was so dark within that he would not know in what direction he would be traveling. He would be hopelessly lost. It was not without reason that it was called the Impenetrable Forest.

But he did have the magic wand and he knew that somehow it would help him. He again withdrew the wand from his belt and pointed it at a huge tree directly in front of him. Nothing happened. Time and again he pointed it at the tree as if jabbing at it with a sword, expecting some sort of magic to again take place. Still nothing happened. Frustrated, he swung the wand against the tree in the manner of a parent who takes a switch to a naughty child. Quite effortlessly the wand passed through the trunk like a knife through butter. The huge tree fell backward to the ground. "So this is how I will penetrate the forest," shouted the prince. With no more effort than the simple swing of his arm, the prince cut a path through the forest. Had he not been in such a hurry to rescue his princess, he might have looked back and noticed that where every tree was felled a new one was quickly growing in its place.

When he emerged from the forest and entered the Land of Yucch, he called to some passers-by to ask if they knew the whereabouts of Princess Purity. When these people saw the path through the woods the prince had just cut, they screamed for joy and hurried past him without answering his query. While there was time they were making a hasty escape from the place. Some others heard the excitement and came running. These, too, upon seeing the path through the Impenetrable Forest, without a word to the hapless prince, made a quick exit. But now the trees were growing back rapidly so that some of the last ones who entered on the path were caught short and lost in the forest. The shouts of elation from those who reached the Shallow River and freedom, and those of anguish from those stranded in the forest, were soon lost to the ears of Prince Gallant as the woods once again became impenetrable.

If the truth were to be told, then it must be said that for all his valor and courage as Prince Gallant stood at the threshold of the Land of Yucch, he was afraid. What manner of terrors would he find here? What awful fate awaited those who unfortunately ended up in this place? He didn't dare ask himself, "Why did I come?"

But his fear soon gave way to confidence as his hand moved slowly down to his belt and he felt the magic wand pressed reassuringly against his body. This land looked no different than the two kingdoms he came from. There were houses scattered throughout the countryside, and here and there he saw several small villages where certainly people would wander about. Thus he knew that he must begin his quest without hesitation, for such is the only course for the valiant.

As he made his way toward the nearest village, he encountered a poorly dressed peasant proceeding slowly toward him, a walking stick directing his steps.

"Good sir!" the prince greeted the stranger. "Can you tell me if you have seen Princess Purity?"

The peasant stopped. "Friend, I have seen no one," was his reply.

"Surely this place is not so great that you could have overlooked someone so fair and lovely as my princess."

"I have overlooked no one, for I have never looked over anyone."

What a strange reply, thought the prince, unable to fathom its meaning. He must remember to ask the Royal Advisor to explain it to him. However, this was not the time for thinking, but for action.

"She stands almost my height," he continued, "and her hair is yellow like the sun and soft as a summer breeze. Her eyes are deep brown like the good, warm earth, and her lips are red like ripe cherries.

"What is red?" asked the peasant.

Again a strange reply, thought the prince. "What is

red?" he repeated. "Red is the color of cherries, the color of apples. Red is the setting sun. Have you never seen the setting sun?"

"Sir, I have never seen anything. I am blind."

"Blind," the prince repeated. "What is blind?"

Now it was the peasant's turn to puzzle over the prince's question. To explain blindness to a sighted person is as strange as explaining sight to a blind person.

"Blind is hardness and softness. It is hot and warm and cold. It is hands that feel and tell."

"But what of color and beauty? You've said nothing of them?"

"I do not know them."

"But you must. You have eyes. I can see you have eyes."

"My eyes cannot see."

"But they are open like mine."

"Mine are closed inside."

The prince was startled, shocked at this new knowledge, for, as you remember, in the Kingdom of the East and West there was no sickness. He struggled to understand, to find meaning.

"The wicked dragon did this to you. I shall rid the land of this monster."

"The dragon did not do this to me. I was born this way."

"How can this be?"

"How can it not be?"

The encounter was too much for the prince to bear—nor should he have had to without his Royal Advisor to advise him. While this stranger presented a challenge greater than any dragon or for that matter any opponent he had ever encountered, he felt that he dare not tarry any longer. His princess awaited him. Thus he politely bid farewell to the blind peasant and continued on his venture. For the first time in his life the prince experienced a feeling he had never known before. He was uncomfortable.

IV

As the prince approached the village he saw a woodsman gathering twigs alongside the road. He called out to him.

"Hello there! Can you help me?"

The man continued gathering wood without paying attention to his call. The prince walked over to the stooped figure whose back was to him.

"Pardon me, good fellow. Can you help me in my search for Princess Purity?"

The woodsman continued his work, totally ignoring the prince's polite request.

"I said, can you help me find my princess?"

There was no response. The woodsman neither stopped his work, nor turned to the prince, nor even acknowledged his presence. How could one continue to be polite in the face of such rudeness? The prince took hold of the peasant's shoulder and with a mighty pull lifted the man and turned him around.

"Answer me when I speak to you," growled the prince, angry at such unaccustomed lack of respect. The woodsman looked in alarm at the raging prince.

"Have you seen Princess Purity?"

The man simply stared blankly, without answering.

"Answer me. I am a prince. I will have you punished if you don't answer me."

The hapless man gave no response. This so infuriated the prince that he began to throttle him violently, all the while shouting at him, "Answer me! "Answer me!"

The woodsman broke free from the prince's grasp. He gestured to his ears and shook his head.

"What is it?" asked the prince.

Again the man pointed to his ears. He then made some incomprehensible guttural sounds.

"You will have to speak more intelligently," the prince said. Suddenly the thought struck him. Perhaps he is speaking a different language, and I don't know any other language. But no, that could not be, for he recalled that the blind man spoke his language. Then that could not possibly be the reason for this man's strange utterances. This land was certainly confusing. Now he was angry that his advisor was not to be found when he had set out on this journey. What was he to do with these strange people? Thoughts of the advisor brought thoughts of the wizard, which in turn reminded him of the magic wand. He unsheathed it from his belt and pointed it at the woodsman. He felt certain this would solve the dilemma.

When the woodsman saw the prince point the wand at him, he thought that it was being offered to him, so he quite nonchalantly took it from the prince and laid it on his woodpile. He nodded his head in gratitude, lifted the bundle to his shoulder and started down the road.

The prince was dumbstruck. "Give me my wand!" he shouted at the retreating figure. Again the woodsman ignored him. He ran up behind him and shouted louder, "Give me back my wand!" It was to no avail. The blind man could not see, he thought. Could it be possible that this man cannot hear? He continued walking along behind him. He decided to test this unbelievable theory. "What ho! You fool!" he shouted. No response. "You cur! You dog! Stand and fight like a man!" No response.

It was true. The man had ears but could not hear, just as the other had eyes but could not see. What a strange land this truly is, he thought. I must rescue my princess and flee from this terrible place. But first, I must retrieve my magic wand.

He hurried to the walking figure and carefully slipped the wand out of his bundle. The woodsman continued on, unaware of what the prince had done.

V

Now the full weight of what this venture would entail pressed itself upon the hapless prince. This was indeed a strange and awful land, far worse in the reality than in the fantasy of childhood imaginings. Fearfulness was always a dragon—but it could be slain. Terribleness was always captivity, a dungeon, a tower room, but there was escape. This place seemed indomitable.

As he traveled from one community to another he progressively passed through stages of shock and disbelief to numbness, dread and finally utter helplessness. Where his people were tall and handsome, here they came in unaccustomed sizes and shapes that were not always pleasant to the eye. Where his people were strong and agile, here they limped and stooped. Where his people were ruddy and full of the vigor of life, here they were pale, drawn and often listless. Were it not for his royal birth, his princely valor and the magic wand which he had taken to clasping more often, he would have left that terrible place, princess or no princess. These were like a shield to him that kept him immune from the dangers that surrounded him. He must find her and soon before the shield was broken or he himself would be irretrievably lost.

He was all but convinced that his quest was hopeless when a one-armed peasant uttered the words that brought back life to his saddened heart.

"She is here," he said simply.

"She is here!" the prince shouted. "She is here?" he repeated as if questioning the credibility of his hearing. "She is here!" he screamed again excitedly.

"She's here! She's here!" he shouted to the heavens in gratitude for his prayers having been heard.

"For God's sake, tell me," he said to the peasant. "Where is she? Where can I find her?"

"In the widow's hut at the edge of the village—but . . ."

Before he could continue the prince rushed off as quickly as his sound limbs could take him. He ran through the village, brushing past scattered groups of people, only pausing long enough to confirm the location of the widow's hut.

When he knocked at the door, he did it with such force that had he continued he would surely have knocked it down. Fortunately the widow opened the door.

"What is it, good sir?" she asked.

"Princess Purity!" he shouted. "Is she here?"

"She is. She is within," she answered, stepping back and pointing to an interior door. Prince Gallant forgot his manners, hurried past the old woman and burst through the door.

It was a bedroom. The room was dark, and his eyes, accustomed to the bright sunlight, did not immediately adjust to the dim light the lamp gave to the room. He stood there as if blind. For a moment he thought that he had at last been striken himself. Was this the accursed doing of the wretched dragon? But slowly his eyes adjusted to the darkness. The princess was standing by the bed of a shabby peasant. She held in her hand a bowl of soup which she was feeding to the old man.

"Purity!" he shouted.

The girl stopped—the spoon suspended midway to the waiting patient. Suddenly the spoon fell from her hands to the earthen floor. She turned quickly around. When the prince saw her he rushed to her side. Dropping to his knees before the startled princess, he embraced her, shouting out, "I've found you! At last I've found you!"

VI

There was so very much for the young couple to recount to each other that the daylight hours passed quickly and the night fire in the fireplace blazed bright on the hearth when the telling was done. The prince brought the reverie to an end with the announcement, "In the morning we will leave this dread place."

The princess was startled by the abruptness of it. It was unexpected, and yet it should not have been, had she been attentive to the full impact of the prince's adventure. It was a tale of valor and heroism and magic in the face of hideous dangers and the awful dragon. It was only logical that he should now wish to rescue his fair princess from her woeful captivity.

However, the princess was so anxious to tell the prince her own story that she had barely listened to his adventure. She had politely waited for appropriate pauses in his narration to interject her own exciting narrative. What appeared to be a dialogue was in truth a tandem monologue.

Nor did the prince listen carefully to the princess' account, else he would not have been as equally surprised by her response when she said: "Leave here? What for?"

"What for? Why to get away from the dreadful dragon. To get away from so many strange people. To go home and be married!"

The prince seemed to be calling the princess back to a world that was long ago and far away. The dreadful dragon? She had not thought about or seen the dragon since he carried her into the Land of Yucch. Marriage? She had forgotten that she was on her way to her betrothal when her misadventure occurred. Strange people?

"What strange people?" she asked aloud.

"Why, people with eyes that don't see and with ears that don't hear. People with big heads and short legs. People with small bodies and people with withered limbs. Never have I seen or imagined that there could ever be such a place as this. We must leave here and at once lest some such evil befall us . . ."

It was difficult for the princess to remember the Kingdom of the East and the people who all looked alike, dressed alike, and acted alike. Had she been in this new land for so long or had so much happened in so short a time that getting all those events together made for twice her previous life? Or was it that each new encounter since she had arrived here was so different from anything she had ever known, each change so much an adventure, each passing day such a new challenge that great lengths of time had bounded by in short, quick, unnoticed leaps? There was no longer the monotonous routine of her previously idyllic life. How different her experience was than that of the prince! He saw these people as strange; she saw them as interesting. He saw them as dreadful; she saw them as challenging. He thought of escape; she thought of living here as rewarding. Her reply could only be, "I cannot leave here."

Once again the prince did not understand what was meant. "You need not worry," he asserted proudly. "I will take care of the dreadful dragon. I have a magic wand." He withdrew it from his belt and displayed it for the princess. "I must admit that I don't always know what it will do," he said "but in some strange way it always manages to work."

"I'm not concerned about the dragon," Princess Purity protested. "But I am concerned about my friends. There is old Thomas here whom I feed every day and who tells me such wonderfully wise and learned things. And there's his sister Anna who shares this hut and their daily fare with me. Yes, and there's David, the blind man. True, his eyes do not see, but he sees more with his ears than most do with their eyes. And Simon, the deaf man, who hears more with his eyes than most do with their ears. There are others, too—so many others. They are my friends and I cannot leave them.

"You cannot *or dare* not?"

A strange rejoinder, thought the princess. "I do not wish to," she clarified.

"You must. It is your duty as a princess to return with me and take your place as my wife."

"But I wish to remain here. Don't you see? I have a new life here. I don't wish to go away."

"No, I don't see. This is not how it should be."

"Listen to me," she pleaded. "I cannot leave what I have found here."

"I will not listen. You have not found here. You have lost here. You have lost your senses. I will take you away from this place. There is some dreadful spell over you. The wicked dragon has done this. I will not listen any longer to your foolish pleadings. Once you are back home in your own kingdom, with your own people, you will see things differently!"

The discussion was over. The finality of it was evident when the prince declared, "We leave at sunrise."

VII

When Prince Gallant awoke the following morning he was deeply disturbed to learn that the princess was gone.

"Gone? What do you mean she's gone?" he asked the old widow.

"She left during the night," she replied, annoyed at her inquisitor.

"Who took her away? Who kidnaped her? Why didn't you call me?" He was shouting at the old woman forgetting all his manners and his royal upbringing. This place was beginning to have its effect on him, and unless he left soon he feared that he too would be hopelessly lost.

"No one took her," the widow snorted. "She left of her own free will."

Such a prospect was too absurd to be true. Why would she ever run away from him? After all, they were to be married. They were to live in a palace and live happily ever after. Why would she refuse to leave this dreadful place? Remembering that she had acted peculiarly during their conversation the night before, he concluded that she must be under a spell. The spell no doubt was the work of the dreadful dragon. What other explanation could there possibly be? He must test his theory on this old woman, but carefully, for she was most likely in league with the dragon.

"She left of her own free will," he repeated her last statement, as if puzzling over it. "But why did she leave?"

"To get away from you."

The old woman's reply was harsh and unyielding. He would have to mellow his questions if he wished to learn anything.

"Why from me? I certainly mean her no harm. Did she not tell you that we are betrothed?"

"She did. But you wish to take her away from here and she has no desire to leave."

"How can this be, since she was on her way to my kingdom for our wedding when she ... she ..."—he stammered momentarily but then quickly continued— "she ventured into this place."

"She has found her place here with us and no longer wishes to leave."

This approach was getting the prince nowhere. He must change course. "You say she left during the night, but there was no moon last night. Did she take a lamp to light her way?"

Cleverly, the prince was laying a trap. He had spent the night keeping watch over the cabin, half wanting to protect the princess and half fearing she would do what she did. Had anyone approached or left the hut carrying a lantern, he could not have failed to notice it while he was on watch.

"She carried no lamp. She needed none. David came to her and helped her away."

"You lie, old hag," he shouted. "Had anyone come during the night I would surely have seen his lamplight. There was none either coming or going, for I kept vigil the whole night through. The princess then must be under a spell as I suspected. How else can she travel at times and in places where others cannot. I have often heard of such spells. Either you have put a spell on her or you are in league with the one who has," he exclaimed, withdrawing his magic wand and brandishing it at her as if it were a sword.

She pushed the wand aside, fearless of its power. "There is no spell, you foolish youth. David is blind. He has no use for lamps. He came to visit last night and heard you stalking about in the woods. He waited until you passed and then came in to warn us of a prowler. Purity explained her problem with you to him, so with his help they left in the dark of the night. What is all this nonsense about spells? If anyone is under a spell, it is you, sir, who would take her away from those she loves and who love her!"

Prince Gallant could not listen any longer. He rushed from the hut angry, hurt and bewildered. He stood facing the vast land before him immobilized with indecision. Then he raised the magic wand high above his head and shouted, "Magic wand, lead me to my princess."

He stood there like a statue—waiting. It was as if the whole world had stopped. Finally, the magic wand slowly moved and pointed to the far mountains.

"She's been taken to the mountains," he screamed in frustration. "She's been taken to the mountains." In a deep breath he gathered together his courage and conviction. "On my oath as a prince, I will let no danger, no evil, no dragon turn me away from my course. I will rescue my princess or die."

VIII

The princess and two companions were hurrying along a narrow mountain pass. To one side of them was a sheer drop down the face of a cliff. The deaf man was leading, with the blind man at the rear. All three kept one hand in constant touch with the mountain wall for security and comfort.

Prince Gallant, younger and stronger than the princess' escorts, quickly caught up to them. He shouted ahead to her. "Purity! Fear not! I will rescue you."

The princess stopped her flight at his call. David and Simon took up a defensive position as bodyguards before her.

"What are you talking about?" she cried out in exasperation. "Rescue me? What do you mean, rescue me? I am fleeing from you."

Her words struck Prince Gallant to the heart. He must not listen. He must not let the evil spell on his princess deter him from his noble duty. For a moment he wished that he were blind so that he would not have to see her look of rejection. For a moment he wished that he were deaf so that he would not have to listen to her cruel and cutting words. It was the accursed dragon's spell for sure, and he must act soon, for it was beginning to affect him.

"Listen to me, Purity," he pleaded. "I have not come to harm you but to save you. I want to save you from this awful place and these hideous people. I know that the dreadful dragon has cast a spell on you, but I have a magic wand and it will help us to safety."

The princess stood there stunned by what he said. What awful place? Why, it was no different from either of their two kingdoms. Hideous people? She had never thought of old Thomas, or the widow Anna, or blind David, or deaf Simon as hideous people. Fury welled up within her.

"It is not I who have a spell on me," she screamed. "It is you who have a spell. It is that magic wand. It keeps you from seeing what you should see and hearing what you should hear."

She could barely talk through the hurt and the tears. There was no more she could say, so she turned to flight. David and Simon held their stance across the path to protect her from her tormentor's pursuit. Prince Gallant drew his magic wand and proceeded up the path to battle them.

At precisely that moment a terrible shriek filled the mountain air and echoed and re-echoed its frightful sound into infinity. Seemingly from nowhere the dreadful dragon appeared in the sky above them. His awful cries rent the mountain stillness like a thousand daggers, over and over again, tearing at every crevice, every cranny, every gully. The prince had to block his ears against the terrible sound of the beast. The princess, seeing that he was thus distracted, continued her flight.

When Prince Gallant moved to resume his pursuit, the dragon began to swoop down on him. He quickly waved the magic wand at his attacker, and once again the wand spewed forth an endless stream of thick smoke. Once again the dragon was thwarted by the dense cloud that quickly covered the mountain pass. The beast bellowed in frustration and rage.

The princess, in the midst of her flight, was overtaken by the rapidly spreading smoke. So quickly did it envelop her that she did not notice that the path ahead turned sharply. She continued going straight and stumbled down the face of the cliff.

Prince Gallant made his way slowly through the smoke toward the princess' defenders. He could neither see because of the smoke nor hear because of the ear-splitting cries of the dragon. It was he who was now at a disadvantage. The blind David who could hear what others could not heard the prince's footsteps between the dragon's bellows. He pointed to Simon where the prince was. Simon, deaf though he was, could see where others could not. He saw the figure of the groping prince and charged him like a battering ram. The prince, caught off-guard, was knocked harshly to the ground. When he stood up to defend himself his attackers retreated into the smoke and the noise. Then with practical cunning they repeated the procedure several more times until eventually the dragon flew off.

The weary prince rose to his feet again, relieved by the sudden silence. Now he would not be caught off-guard by his attackers, for the smoke was lifting and he would be able to defend himself. Just ahead of him he could see his two tormentors. He reached for his magic wand, but it was gone. He must have dropped it when he was battered to the ground. Anyway, there was no time to look for it, for the combatants were approaching. This would be a battle to the death.

It was the blind man who heard it first. He stopped and held out a restraining hand to his companion. He put his finger before his mouth in a gesture to keep silent. The deaf man froze in his tracks. Even the prince stood still, startled by this sudden strange turn of events!

David lifted his head like an animal sniffing the breeze, listening intently. He heard it again. Only this time it was a little louder so that the others too perked their ears attentively. It was part moan and part cry. It was the princess and she was in trouble.

Princess Purity had fallen to a ledge just below the mountain path. The fall had temporarily dazed her. As she regained her senses and saw the danger she was in, she began to cry out in distress: "Help! Help me! Someone please help me!"

There could not be combat between the men now that the princess was in distress. The three of them hurried up the path to the bend in the road. Prince Gallant looked down the precipice. Some ten feet below them lay the princess. He called down to her.

"I'm here, Purity. I'm here. Don't worry. I'll save you."

"Hurry! Please hurry!" she cried. "I'm so afraid. This ledge won't hold me."

No sooner did she say that when the precarious ledge began to rumble beneath her. It was beginning to break away from the cliff.

"What can I do?" the prince cried out to himself. "There's no time to go back and look for the magic wand."

David and Simon both stared down the cliff face equally lost in bewilderment. The princess was stranded below their reach.

"Where is my advisor?" Prince Gallant screamed. "Now that I really need him, where is he?" These are precisely the times when princes' have advisors and counselors to guide them. But he was alone. The princess' cries reached up to him, tormenting him. What could he do? In nervousness and frustration his hands fiddled with the loose ends of the sash wrapped belt-like around his waist. Over and over he looped them distractedly as if the motion could somehow crank out a solution. Instead of a solution, he had tied the sash into a massive knot.

Then it struck him. But he would need help. David and Simon stood facing him, anguished by their helplessness.

"Help me!" he shouted to them. "We must form a chain."

They did not understand him. Prince Gallant explained his idea by pointing to the knots in his sash and motioning that the three of them could link themselves together as a chain in order to reach the princess. At last they understood.

Removing the sash from around his waist, Prince Gallant tied David's feet to a tree growing near the edge of the cliff. David stretched his body full length on the ground face down and extended his arms as far as possible in front of him. The prince then tied Simon's feet to David's wrists, and then his feet to Simon's wrists. They were now a human chain. Slowly, carefully, they lowered themselves toward the princess.

"Remain calm," the prince soothed as he inched his way agonizingly toward her. "In just a moment I'll be there. Don't move!"

But the tension was too much for the princess to bear. She jumped to her feet to reach out for the prince's hand. The sudden movement caused the ledge to give way. In a moment she would plummet to her death.

"Jump!" he screamed. Instinctively she obeyed. The prince stretched out with all his strength and caught her by the hand. The sound of falling rocks echoed throughout the chasm below.

IX

Many years passed. Prince Gallant married Princess Purity and they were kept very busy raising their fourteen children. They never did return to their native lands. The prince agreed with the princess that it was far more interesting, not to mention exciting, in this new home.

It would be nice to end by saying that they lived happily ever after, but that would be expecting too much of the Land of Yucch, especially with that many children. After all, this is not a fairy tale.

As to what happened to the magic wand—Prince Gallant brought it back down the mountain with him but for some strange reason it never seemed to work again—except when the children became unruly. Then Princess Purity knew exactly how to use it, and the villagers said that it worked like magic.

Ugly Bird

Once upon a time there was an ugly bird. She was quite different from all the other birds in the kingdom. Where some birds had beautiful, colorful plumage, her feathers were short and dull. Where some birds had long, slender legs and walked gracefully, hers were short and stubby. Where some could fly and soar through the heavens with great majesty, she could only walk the earth and scratch its dust. Where some sang beautiful songs that filled the air with sweet music, she could only peep annoyingly. Alas, indeed she was an ugly bird.

The other birds felt quite put out by Ugly Bird. She was a disgrace and a blight to their species. "Something should be done," they agreed. "Send her to the physicians. Perhaps they can do something." And so they did.

Try as they might, the physicians could do nothing to improve Ugly Bird's condition. They could not make her feathers long or colorful. They could not make her

legs more graceful, nor could they make her voice sweet and pretty. Their conclusion was that she would always remain an ugly bird.

The news filled Ugly Bird with great sadness. To think she would never be able to fly or sing or strut proudly like a peacock. She was not only ugly, but she felt utterly useless. The more she thought about her sad state of affairs, the more depressed she became. Her sadness became heavier and heavier. It knotted up like a ball weighing heavily in the pit of her stomach. When it became so heavy that she could no longer bear it, she began to cry and squalk uncontrollably.

When the doctors who had been pondering her case heard the commotion, they came running to her assistance. What they found filled them with great amazement! There beneath Ugly Bird was the most beautiful, the most magnificent egg they had ever seen! Immediately, others were called to witness this great phenomenon. From there the news spread quickly throughout the whole kingdom. Ugly Bird could lay the most magnificent eggs the world had ever seen.

Thus the chicken, a bird that cannot fly or sing, that is by far the ugliest bird in the kingdom, has given to mankind one of its greatest gifts . . . the egg!

Masks

A man sat at a dressing room table gazing intently at himself in the mirror. His face was the picture of comedy with its wide, open-mouthed grin and big empty eyes. He rose and exited the room, entering a long corridor with doors to rooms on either side. He entered the first door.

The room was filled with the sounds of a happy party. There were clusters of people laughing, some gesturing animatedly in lively conversation, others drinking contentedly, and still others singing discordantly to the music that blared in the background. As the man mingled among the various groups he blended in easily and inconspicuously, for every person at the party wore the same mask of comedy that he had. He wandered for a while from group to group but eventually left to return to his seat before the mirror.

Once again he stared at his reflection, but more deeply, more pensively. He scrutinized carefully every part of his face. At the base of his neck, at the hollow

beneath his Adam's apple, he saw a thin, almost invisible line circle the length of his neck. He put his hands to his neck, testing the line along the soft sensitive underside of his fingers to make sure that it was really there. Then slowly with his thumbs he began rubbing upward until the skin began to roll, breaking away from the rest of the torso. But it was not skin at all. It was rubber and he was unwittingly removing from his face a mask.

When he was done he again looked at himself in the mirror. Once again there were the wide, hollow, empty eyes. Only now his mouth grimaced downward in sadness. His face was the mask of tragedy.

Again he proceeded into the corridor, now opening the next door. Here the room was filled with mourners, people who wailed and cried unceasingly. The music was unmistakenly dirge-like and the atmosphere was overwhelmingly funereal. He wandered among the people, blending inconspicuously once again, for like himself all the others wore the mask of tragedy. He remained but a short time. Then he returned to his mirror.

Once again scrutiny revealed a thin line at the base of his neck. This too he tested and, in the same way he had done before, he removed the mask.

This time when he looked at his face he was terribly shocked by what the mirror reflected. He had no face at all. Where his eyes, nose and mouth should be there was nothing at all. His face was a conical blank.

The man was seized with an instant terror. He took hold of the mask of comedy which lay on the dressing table and put it on over his head. It no longer fit. Now it hung loosely, unable to be drawn snugly back into place. He threw it off for the mask of tragedy but the result was the same. The old mask no longer fit.

He could not bear to look at an empty face, so he stumbled out of the room and back into the corridor. This time he entered yet another room

Here the room was more lively. Once again party music filled the air while groups of people mingled with one another in pleasant conversation. The man broke in on the first group.

It was difficult to say who was more startled. The man was awestruck by the overwhelming beauty of each person there. Never had he seen more handsome men or more incredibly beautiful women. But they were dumbstruck by the presence of one with no face.

The awkwardness, however, lasted but a few minutes. Seeing that the hapless man had no face, the beautiful people proceeded at once to give him one. One colored in eyes and another lips. He was given a thin and aquiline nose which was really quite becoming. His face was beautiful. He wandered over to another group. Here again he was overwhelmed by the startling beauty of the people. When these saw what the others had done to the face of the man, they too wished to join in the sport. His wide eyes were erased for more seductive ones, and his nose was slightly widened for a more masculine look with just a slight upturn at the tip so as not to appear harsh.

The next beautiful group was more interested in his mouth and ears but again had to rearrange his eyes and nose to fit the new demeanor.

At last it became too much for the man. He wandered dejectedly back to his own room. His old discarded masks still lay on the dressing table, and he tossed them aside in frustration. He sat at the mirror and wiped off the last traces of what the beautiful people had painted on him. He was once again faceless.

Then as if suddenly remembering something, he began rummaging through each of the table's drawers. Unable to find whatever it was he was looking for, he began searching the room. Still unsuccessful, he opened the closet door. There on the top shelf, behind old and discarded things, he found it. It was another mask. This mask had a face. It was the face of Jesus.

Thoughtfully, almost prayerfully, he put on the mask and returned to the mirror. It was a perfect fit—so perfect in fact that he couldn't find the thin line that betrayed its presence.

With his new-found mask, he left his room and re-entered the first door.

When the happy people took notice of his presence they became strangely uncomfortable. Even though the man felt comfortably happy with his new mask it seemed that those in the room found it strangely sad and quite unlike their own. With open-mouthed grins they admonished him to grin the way they did so that he would fit in. But he felt that he was grinning and told them so. They quickly became infuriated at his obstinacy and uncooperativeness, all the while smiling eerily at him. Before long the smiling faces chased him angrily out of the room. He escaped them by entering the next room.

The next room proved to be no different and hence no refuge from his pursuers. Here too they admonished him not to smile, since they were all in mourning. Despite his protestation that he was in sympathy with them, his face reflected more serenity than sadness. He was run out of the room and back into the corridor where the others awaited him. Once more he evaded them by bolting through the third door.

The beautiful people greeted him with the same irritation as the others had. His face was not beautiful, he was told, and therefore he had no right being in the room. He answered by saying something about beauty being only skin deep, which only served to infuriate them the more. To a person they turned on him, so he fled the room before they could take hold of him.

But there was no safety to be found in the corridor. His pursuers from the other two rooms awaited him. With his progress blocked and retreat impossible, he was set upon by the frenzied mob. They beat him savagely until his body slumped at their feet—lifeless.

Showing no emotion other than the masks they wore—comedy, tragedy, beauty—one of their number reached down and removed the mask from their fallen victim. He tore off the face of Jesus and cast it aside.

The emotion that suddenly overwhelmed them was

not expressed through facial features but through instinctive bodily motions. Every one of them recoiled a step backward, at the same time throwing one or both arms across their faces to shield from their eyes the sight before them.

Underneath the mask of Jesus the dead man bore the face of Jesus. Not a word was spoken. Not a sound was heard.

Then to the utter amazement and terror of them all, the dead man quietly and quite nonchalantly rose and walked away down the corridor.

Gradually the crowd dispersed and slowly re-entered the rooms they had come from—all except one. He bore the mask of tragedy. He instead entered the first room and sat on the chair facing the dressing table mirror. He looked at himself closely, pensively. During this scrutiny he looked curiously at a thin almost imperceptible line at the base of his neck.

The Encounter:
A Tale of Love

Once upon a time, somewhere in the magic world of fairy tales, there were two kingdoms—the kingdom of Shaylo and the kingdom of Tayra. Now the kings and queens of these two kingdoms decided to hold a royal celebration to honor the thousand years of friendship that had existed between them. It was to be a celebration the likes of which had never been seen before or ever would be again. Everyone was invited to attend, from the greatest to the least and from every corner of the two lands.

Everyone was invited, even Draga, the witch of the West. But she would have none of it, since the idea was not to her liking, especially because it was not of her own making. When the plans proceeded without her, she fumed with a mighty fury and vowed a terrible vengeance if the occasion were to take place.

The great festivity did take place, and everyone

was there in celebration, when, in the midst of the merriment, Draga appeared.

"A curse on both your houses," she shrieked. "A curse on both your houses. It will come on a day and at a time you least expect. My wrath is like the lion; it will devour you."

With the malediction uttered, she disappeared with the sun in the western sky.

From that day forward, all the peoples of both kingdoms made certain to bolt all the windows and close all the shutters that face west when the sun was about to set, for they were certain that this would be the time she would seek her vengeance. They would be on their guard.

And so they were for many years. It became a daily ritual in the kingdoms for the people to shutter their west windows every evening at sundown. The kings of both kingdoms made it a royal decree so that no one might perchance forget and unwittingly allow the witch entrance into the kingdoms. Just before sunset, soldiers would pass through the villages and towns announcing "The sun is setting; bar the west windows. The sun is setting; bar the west windows."

If not for that nightly reminder, the incident of the witch would have all but been forgotten. The kingdoms continued on their activities in peace and merriment.

The king and queen of Shaylo gave birth to a son, while the king and queen of Tayra gave birth to a daughter. It was said that they were the two most beautiful children anyone had ever seen.

Manfried grew to be a dashing, handsome and brave, young prince, and Elsinora was a beautiful and graceful princess. It was no surprise to anyone of either kingdom when they announced their betrothal. They were a magnificent couple, and the wedding feast was compared in grandeur second only to the great feast once held by both their houses.

The love of Manfried and Elsinora was renowned. Never had two more beautiful people shown such a great love for one another. They were in every way a prince and princess.

The news of the birth of their firstborn child, Manuel, brought great rejoicing throughout the lands. The day of the christening was announced, and, as was the custom, a royal celebration was to follow.

Everyone was busy in preparation for the occasion. Elsinora sat before the castle window sewing Manuel's baptismal gown while Manfried made final preparations with his minister of affairs.

A strange sweet smell of delicate flowers wafted through the window near the spot where Elsinora was working. The lovely scent drew her attention from her sewing. She rose and went to the window to breathe in more fully the sweet smell of the spring blossoms. The sun had just begun its downward journey. In the distance, the call of the soldiers' warning was lost in the rapture of the moment.

Elsinora called to her husband. "Manfried, come and see how sweet the spring air smells."

Manfried walked to her side. "We must shutter the window, dear, for the sun is setting."

"Only for a moment. Breathe this delightful perfume."

Manfried breathed in deeply, and the sweet fragrance captured his senses. He was mesmerized. So, too, was Elsinora. The sweet perfume had lulled them into a waking sleep. While they stood there thus lulled, the sun set in the west.

Suddenly, a violent cold wind blew through the window. Manfried and Elsinora were startled into wakefulness, both by the chill of the wind and the scream of the nurse. The scream returned and echoed throughout the castle. "He's gone. He's gone. He's gone."

Manfried ran up the stairs to the boy's bedroom in a bound, Elsinora close behind him.

The nurse pulled at her hair and cried uncontrollably: "She took him. That awful witch took him."

"What happened?"

"My lord, forgive me."

"Tell me what happened," he shouted, shaking the hysterical woman.

"Young Manuel lay sleeping, and I, in my chair, was watching. Sir, a sweet smell of flowers filled the air, and I began to doze in slumber—but only for a moment. Soon I felt a cold chill surround my body, and then I noticed her—that awful witch. She stood there over the crib and took the child. I jumped to stop her. She put out her hand against me. The touch of that witch was like the touch of death. Cold as ice, it was. It was the touch of death, I tell you, the touch of death."

"Then what happened?" Manfried shouted at her.

"She went to the window and opened the shutters. I could see the sun setting just in front of her. Then she was gone. She flew out the window and was gone. She took Manuel with her."

The mention of the boy reminded her of her plight. "My God," she screamed. "Manuel is gone. The boy is gone."

The news spread throughout the kingdoms. The kings and queens of Shaylo and Tayra hastened to the stricken castle to offer their children solace and comfort.

"There is but one hope," they told the bereaved couple. "The goodly wizard of the East. Only he can provide an answer to this tragedy."

"How are we to find him?" asked Manfried.

"We will wait for him. He comes to those who look for him when the first rays of the sun shine on us out of the eastern sky."

So the royal families went to the parapet of the highest tower of the castle and awaited the sunrise.

As they had hoped, so it happened. The first ray of sunlight from the east brought the good wizard. He stood bathed in light, radiant as the sun which blazed behind him.

"Good wizard," Manfried said, "the wicked witch of the West has taken our son. What are we to do?"

"Who allowed this evil to happen?" he asked.

"We did," admitted Manfried and Elsinora.

"Your folly will cost you dearly. I must tell you that the witch has plans to slay the child. This she will do three days hence."

"No!" screamed Elsinora.

"I will stop her," shouted the prince drawing out his sword. "With a mighty army I will rout the witch from her castle and kill the beast. By all that is in me, I will rescue my child."

"No army will take her, nor will your sword. Nor will all that is within you save the boy. It can be done, but it will cost you—both of you, for it was the folly of both of you that brought this tragedy."

"No matter the cost, we will pay it," shouted Manfried.

"We will," affirmed Elsinora.

"Then come with me," said the wizard. He took each by the hand, and as quickly as the sun's rays streak across the sky, they found themselves at the foot of a high mountain. There, at the top, was the castle of the wicked witch of the West.

"Manuel is up there," announced the good wizard. "The witch is away doing her evil but will return in three days. When she does, she will slay the child."

"Tell me what I must do," begged Elsinora.

"Listen," said the wizard:

"To have is not to have.

To hold is not to hold.

To each a magic ring to break the power of the king.

To die then is to live forever."

The wizard vanished, leaving Manfried and Elsinora each with a magic ring.

"What are we to do?" asked the princess. "I do not understand. His words made no sense!"

"There is so little time. See, the sun is beginning to sink in the west. There is no time to solve riddles. But we each have a magic ring. Let us call upon its magic to rescue our son."

"Yes," cried Elsinora, "but let us hurry. What should we do?"

Manfried looked at the mountain. "We could climb the mountain, but I'm afraid it might take too long. We have the magic rings. Let us use them."

Manfried held his ring up before him with his hand outstretched so that the sun shone through the ring.

"Magic ring," he cried, "fly me to my son." In an instant, the ring became a mighty bird, bigger than any bird in either kingdom, mighty and majestic like a giant eagle. Manfried was startled by what happened. He no longer held the ring in his hand. Instead, he held a claw of the bird. With a mighty shriek, the giant bird spread and beat its wings, lifting Manfried off the ground.

Elsinora stood there startled and frightened. The eagle was carrying the prince out of sight. She could hear him shout down to her, "I shall save Manuel. Fear not. I shall rescue him." The bird carrying the prince flew around the mountain and out of sight.

Elsinora stood there alone and frightened. What was she to do? She could not just wait, for the sun was in its setting. She thought: "What can I do to ransom my son from that awful witch? Ransom! That's it! Ransom! I must ransom him from the witch." She held the magic ring out to the setting sun and cried out, "Magic ring, bring me a king's ransom." At once, the ring in her hand changed into a huge sack of gold. The great weight of it forced her arm down, crashing to earth with an enormous thud. The princess looked at her treasure and knew what she must do. She must scale the mountain. With all her frail strength, she lifted the sack over her shoulder and began her ascent. Her progress was slow and difficult, and the setting sun brought her welcome relief.

The sun was high in the sky when she awoke. The heaviness of her task had tired her more than she expected. She had overslept. Now she knew she must hurry or lose another day. There were just two days remaining, and much of this day was lost. She lifted her treasure and continued her ascent. There was no time to stop, no time to eat. She must continue on without rest. But the treasure weighed heavily against her progress. Her steps became shorter and shorter until she could proceed no further. She stopped to rest in a clearing before another cliff wall. The sight of the cliff before her seemed overwhelming. Only the thought of rescuing her son could spur her on her quest. But for a moment she knew that she had to rest.

In the midst of her repose, a strange and disturbing sound brought her to her feet. She listened attentively and when she heard what sounded like breathing, heavy breathing, she began to tremble. If only Manfried were with her. Quite suddenly, she heard the sound of heavy footsteps approaching her through the woods. The earth shook with each footstep. Trees were cracking in the still mountain air. There were loud snorts, and then suddenly there emerged a dragon—a fearful, awesome dragon. He sniffed the air, testing, looking. Then he saw her. With a roar of fire and smoke, he started toward the princess.

Elsinora was terrified by the dragon, and she ran to the cliff wall in fright. But then she remembered the ransom, so she hurried back to retrieve the sack. It seemed so heavy she could hardly carry it. When she arrived back at the cliff, the dragon was drawing dangerously close. She started to climb, but the treasure weighed her down and hampered her progress. She reached up to a ledge above her just as the dragon arrived at the cliff and stretched his head up to her. The treasure was too heavy for her to lift herself to safety. At that moment, she heard the words of the good wizard, "To have is not to have." The treasure kept her from safety. If she kept it, the dragon would devour her. But if she dropped it, how would she rescue her son? The answer came, but none too quickly. Elsinora dropped the treasure-laden sack, and it fell into the dragon's open mouth. While he stopped to consume his catch, Elsinora pulled herself to the safety of the ledge. She struggled to the mountain wall, gasping out of fear and exhaustion. In her hand was once again the magic ring.

Manfried woke from a fitful sleep. As the sun began to set, the eagle flew to its nest, in spite of his efforts to spur the bird onward to the top of the mountain. He could do nothing but sleep. Now as he awoke, he saw that the giant bird was gone. He waited impatiently, since the time for rescuing his son was passing all too quickly. He thought of climbing out of the nest, but it lay nestled in a small fissure, with sheer rock wall above and below it. There was no exit from here except the way he came. He must wait for the eagle.

While he waited, he heard a commotion below him—a strange sound. He listened. It was the sound of heavy snorting, followed quickly by the cracking sound of breaking trees. The sound was crisp and clear in the mountain air. Manfried climbed to the top of the nest and peered out. Below him, he saw the dragon emerge from the woods. He watched the dragon sniff the air and thought to himself, "He must be looking for something or someone." He remembered that dragons eat people. Then he looked and saw Elsinora. He screamed out to her, "Elsinora, Elsinora," but she could not hear him. He wanted to jump down to her, but there was no way he could reach her. It was hopeless. He cried out in agony and frustration. At once the eagle reappeared. Before it could settle in its nest, Manfried grabbed hold of a claw. With his sword, he poked at the bird, prodding it on. The giant eagle flew toward where the dragon was still in pursuit of Elsinora who was trapped on the ledge. The eagle hovered above the ledge. Elsinora saw Manfried and cried out to him, "Manfried, help me." Manfried, with one hand still clutching the bird's claw, the other wielding the sword poking at it, could not get the bird to descend any lower. The shrieks of the bird and the dreadful snorts of the dragon terrified the princess all the more.

Suddenly, Manfried remembered the words of the good wizard. "To hold is not to hold." So long as he held on to the eagle, he could not save his wife. But if he released the bird, he might not rescue his son. "To hold is not to hold." He let go of the eagle and fell to the ledge where Elsinora cowered away from the dragon. In his hand once again was the magic ring.

Elsinora embraced Manfried. "We must hurry," he said. "There is still time before the sun sets." Carefully

Manfried walked along the ledge, holding Elsinora's hand and leading the way. The narrow ledge wound around the mountain slowly but steadily higher. As the sun was about to set, the path ended.

The morning sun revealed a deep crack in the mountain wall. The chasm was too big to jump across. The castle was just above them. Manfried stood before his plight angry and frustrated. "What are we to do?" Elsinora cried. "We must think. The wizard's riddle will tell us."

Elsinora then repeated the riddle:

"To have is not to have.

To hold is not to hold

To each a magic ring to break the power of the king."

"To each a magic ring to break the power of the king," interrupted Manfried. He took out his ring. "Break," he repeated. "Break. Are we to break the ring?" Elsinora took out her ring. "But what good would that do?"

"I don't know, but somehow I know both of us must break our rings. Trust me."

Manfried took his ring and shattered it against the mountain. It fell to pieces at his feet. "Now yours," he said, looking at Elsinora. She shattered hers against the mountain, and it too fell to pieces at her feet. As the broken pieces of the two rings fell together on the path, magic suddenly began to happen. The pieces began to wiggle like little worms. Then the pieces got longer and longer until they fused together and became a long golden rope.

Manfried took the rope and lassoed a branch of a tree across the chasm. "I will go on to save Manuel," he told Elsinora.

139

"No," she cried. "When we set out apart, we got nowhere. I know deep inside we must go together. Please trust me. I'm not afraid."

Manfried took Elsinora in his arms. As she held tightly to him, he grabbed hold of the rope and swung across the abyss to the other side.

They proceeded together to the top of the mountain. Before them was the witch's castle. "We must hurry now," Manfried said. They ran forward. The sweet smell of spring flowers filled the air.

"Hold your breath," Manfried shouted. They ran together, holding hands, through the field of flowers that perfumed the mountain air. They ran but held their breaths. Breathless, they arrived at the castle's drawbridge. A cold wind suddenly chilled the air. In the west, the sun was in its rapid descent.

"Wait here. I will open the gate," Manfried shouted. Spurred on by the energy of a man frantic to save his child, Manfried readily scaled the castle wall. However, once inside, seven deadly giants awaited him. In the center of the courtyard was a crib with the child, Manuel, inside. The sun was fading fast in the west.

Manfried stood there alone. There was no magic to help him—no wizard, no ring, just him and his sword. He drew his sword and approached the giants. He fought furiously and wildly, and one giant fell, then another and another. He was wounded and bleeding, yet still he fought on. The fourth and fifth giants fell. His strength was nearly gone, but he continued on. When the sixth giant fell, he had no strength left to fight the seventh. With his mighty sword, the seventh giant ran him through. Manfried fell to the ground.

Outside Elsinora cried out frantically, "Manfried! Manfried!" The shouting drew the giant's attention. He raised his sword, ran to the gate, lifted the crossbar and pushed open the portals.

Elsinora had expected Manfried. The sight of the giant immobilized her with fear. The giant drew his sword and proceeded to her.

Manfried lay gasping his last. He heard the cries of his son, then looked and saw the giant approaching the princess with drawn sword. With all the life and strength that was left in him, he picked up his fallen sword and hurled it like a spear at the unsuspecting giant. The javelin found its mark. The giant slumped to his knees, then fell face downward before Elsinora.

The princess ran to her fallen husband and knelt at his lifeless body, weeping. There, in Manfried's eye, was a tear—a tear born of love, anguish, dread, hope, an unfinished tear, a tear stopped by death. Elsinora looked at that precious tear. She saw reflected in it the sun—the bright and glorious sun. As in a mirror, Elsinora saw the sun set in Manfried's tear. A cold chill gripped her. "My son," she shouted and turned to the crib.

In front of her stood the wicked witch of the West. Before she could utter a cry, the witch struck her down with a mighty blow. Her lifeless body fell atop her husband's. In death, their faces touched each other in an everlasting kiss.

The witch then turned to the child sobbing in its crib.

"At last I am to be avenged," she shrieked. "At last I win."

A tear in the eye of Elsinora slowly made its way down the side of her face. It hung for a moment at the edge of her cheek. Then, gently, it dropped down to the face of Manfried. It fell on the tear that lingered in his eye. The teardrop grew larger and larger. In a moment, in a flash, it became a river, a torrent flowing out of the two dead lovers.

The unsuspecting witch was suddenly swept off her feet as the castle courtyard filled with the rising water. Caught off her guard, the witch struggled in the torrent, but then drowned.

The crib with Manuel in it floated harmlessly above the vortex. The waters began to pour out the castle gate and gently, like a river, down the mountain. The crib, like a boat, traveled down the mountain to the kingdom below. There, the kings and queens of Tayra and Shaylo awaited. The sight of the child brought great rejoicing to them and all the kingdom. Manuel grew to be a strong and fine prince. It is known and voiced about both kingdoms that Manuel will live forever.

The Juggler

Lord, give me your eyes so I can see as you see.
Lord, give me your heart, so I can love as you love.

Today I saw a juggler. He was really a marvelous sight. He balanced twirling plates at the end of long sticks resting on his nose, his forehead and his hands. This he did while twirling a large hoop around his waist and rings around his arms and thighs and calves. He was a marvelous picture of precision, co-ordination and balance. One false move and the plates would come crashing down. One misstep and the rings would fall clattering to the stage. But there were none—no false moves, no missteps. He stood there, a picture of symmetry in motion. The audience applauded, applauded and applauded.

Lord, give me your eyes so that I can see as you see. Let me see that you are a juggler, that you balance

in one grand act an entire universe—planets, stars, moons, and constellations—a marvelous picture of precision and coordination.

With your head, you hold up the sky.

On your feet the earth rests.

In your hands are the mountain heights and the depths of the sea.

Like a twirling hoop all creatures are set in motion by you and around you—the regal lion, the soaring eagle, the lowly, laboring ant.

And in your heart you balance man. Man, tall and mighty; man, small and weak; man, black and brown and white and red and yellow! Young and old. Soon to die and soon to birth.

Lord, give me your eyes so that I can see that everything twirls around you. Everything spins with you at the center. All symmetry, all balance depends on you. One false move, one misstep, one careless diversion and all would come tumbling down. But there are none. You are a picture of beauty and symmetry in motion.

Lord, give me your heart so that I can applaud and applaud and applaud.

Today I saw a child blow up a balloon. His breath gave it life. It was a formless, purposeless mass of rubber before he blew into it. But as his breath entered, it began to grow and take on shape. It got bigger and bigger. Round and puffy ears popped out and a bulbous nose filled in. Soon a dimpled neck appeared and eventually a big round pot belly took shape. When he was finished the balloon looked like a snowman. He tossed it into the air and it tumbled slowly down. Before it hit the ground he caught it gently and tossed it up again. A soft breeze blew it to where children were playing nearby. They scurried around it, laughing and giggling and clapping with joy.

Lord, give me your eyes so that I can see as you see. Let me see that man is a formless, purposeless mass until you breathed your life into him. Your Holy Spirit gives him shape. In his mother's womb you formed him. It was there that he began to take his shape. You breathed and he got bigger and bigger. Round ears popped and a button nose. Soon there was a dimpled chin and a big round belly. When you were finished he looked like a man. You tossed him gently into the world and he was caught in the loving hands of mankind. Your breath blew like a breeze and he tumbled slowly through childhood and youth, adolescence and old age.

Lord, give me your heart so that I can laugh and

giggle and clap with joy at the balloon you have blown in our midst.

Today I saw a party, with children singing and laughing and playing games. A big balloon came floating in their midst carried aloft on a gentle breeze. They jumped and grabbed at it, each time hitting it higher into the air. It flew up to a stage where the juggler balanced his plates and rings. It was a happy sight—the controlled discipline of the juggler and the casual tumbling of the balloon as it floated downward amid the laughter and joy of children.

Slowly it floated down, ever so slowly toward little arms and hands outstretched. There, in one hand, a little higher than all the rest, pinched tightly between thumb and forefinger—a PIN!

Down came the spirit-filled balloon. Up went the hand-held pin. POW!

The laughing ceased, the giggles stopped, the joy ended.

The noise startled the juggler. The plates came crashing down. The rings rolled in confusion around the stage.

The balloon lay on the ground, a formless, purposeless mass.

Lord, give me your eyes so that I can see what we've done.
Lord, give me your heart so that I can cry.

Tiny John:
A Christmas Fable

Once upon a time there lived a little shepherd boy by the name of Tiny John. He was indeed a very tiny boy. Even when he was born he was much smaller than his brothers and sisters were when they were born. The moment his father first saw him he scolded his wife for having such a little baby. "He'd better grow up big," the shepherd said, "or he won't be any good to watch over the sheep."

But he didn't grow up. Rather, he didn't grow up big. He was so small everyone called him Tiny John.

Year after year Tiny John hoped that he would grow big and tall like other children, but year after year he hardly grew at all. His father didn't want him around because he was too small to take care of the sheep. If a wolf were to come along he would certainly not be afraid of Tiny John. His mother didn't want him around because he was too small to do chores. He couldn't cut wood or churn butter or carry things or fix things. She said he was useless around the house. His brothers and sisters didn't like him because they had to do what Tiny John couldn't do. Because of him they had more work to do, so they would get even by calling him names and making fun of him.

One winter evening Tiny John was sitting in front of his house, as usual playing by himself. Even though there were so many stars out they were not enough to warm the night or his spirits. He periodically rubbed his hands together to try to keep warm. He wore only a frayed tunic which did little to protect him against the night chill. His brothers had more clothes, and warmer ones, but they needed them for when they watched the sheep at night. Since Tiny John was too small to do chores he didn't get any extra clothes. Just one tunic—that's all he had.

While he sat there playing he was startled by a great commotion. His father and brothers were running toward the house shouting excitedly. Behind them, running wildly, came the sheep. His mother and sisters ran from the house to see what the trouble was. The boys kept interrupting each other trying to relay the news, which only added to the confusion. Finally, the shepherd told everyone to be quiet while he explained what had happened.

"The boys and I took the sheep over the hill toward Bethlehem," he said. "The night was so cold we started a fire to keep warm. It struck me how especially quiet the night seemed to be. As a matter of fact, I don't ever remember a night being so quiet. There was no noise anywhere—no wind blowing, no trees moving. Even the sheep just lay there quietly. Then one of the boys noticed a bright star in the sky. We were all looking at it, remarking how strange it was both in color and appearance, when it suddenly seemed to fall earthward. As it did it got bigger. And the bigger it got the brighter it became, until it was so bright that the night was lighter than any day I've ever seen. Then singing began to fill the air—beautiful singing. There were angels singing—hundreds of them, thousands of them. We were all so frightened that we fell to the ground and hid our eyes. As we lay there trembling I heard a voice say, 'Get up! Don't be afraid.' I looked up and saw an angel standing before me. He was dressed all in white, and he shone so brightly that I knew instantly that he must have been that star.

" 'What is it? What is happening?' I asked. 'I have good news,' he said. 'Today in Bethlehem a king is born. He is the great king the world has awaited. He is the Christ, the Son of God. Hurry to all your friends and tell them to hasten to Bethlehem to see the new king and do him homage.' When the angel finished speaking he began to float up into the heavens. The higher he ascended the brighter he became, until once again he was a great star in the night sky."

The shepherd was trembling when he finished the story. His family stared at him and then at the star in open-mouthed wonderment. The chills that raced through Tiny John's body were no longer from the cold but from awe.

"We must hurry," the shepherd shouted, breaking the spell. "We must tell the people of our village. We must go to Bethlehem to see this new king."

The boys ran off in one direction and the girls in another. "Tell them to bring gifts too," the shepherd

shouted after them. "After all," he said to his wife as
they hurried inside, "it is only proper that we bring
gifts to our new king."

Before long the whole village was stirring with excitement. People were running about everywhere,
shouting the good news to one another. "Hurry!" they
cried back and forth. "Bring gifts—beautiful gifts for a
king."

The shepherd and his family were making ready
too. The shepherd selected two of his best sheep. His
wife basketed some bread and cakes she had made that
day. Even the children were looking for things to
bring—all the children, that is, except Tiny John. He
had nothing. He owned nothing. There was not a thing

150

that he could find to bring to the newborn king. Never had his isolation or poverty or loneliness weighed so heavily on him as at that moment. But there was no time for regret. A procession of villagers was making its way to the door of his house. The townspeople, laden with their quick-found treasures, gathered to hear from the shepherd himself his tale of wonder.

Once again he recounted the marvelous story to the delight and astonishment of his listeners, and once again Tiny John found his flesh tingling with excitement. But he had nothing to bring. He had no gift.

When the tale was ended the procession resumed, making its way toward the caves of Bethlehem over which the strange new star shone brightly. It left in its wake, standing alone and lonely, Tiny John. Sadness and excitement struggled mightily in his tiny body. To give in to sadness would mean to remain behind and miss this great wonder which was now taking place. But to go meant to be embarrassed once again for not having a gift for the king. There was no happy solution to his dilemma.

They were almost out of sight when he finally decided what he would do. He would join the others. He was Tiny John, was he not? Then no one would even notice him, let alone notice that he bore no gift. For once his size would be to his advantage. He ran as fast as he could to catch up with the procession.

The shepherds and townspeople made their way to the singular cave over which the new star shone brightly. "This is it," they whispered to one another. "The new king must be here." Reverence for nobility had instinctively subdued their peasant caterwauling. Quietly and respectfully they entered the cave.

To their astonishment, already within were three

151

elegantly dressed kings. The third king was presenting his gifts to a peasant couple standing in the corner of the stable. At their feet lay gold and frankincense. After placing his gift before them, he prostrated himself before a manger. Within the manger was a baby. This was the newborn king whose birth was marked by the star and heralded by angels.

Silently the shepherds entered the cave. One by one they approached the crib to see the baby and present their humble gifts. There were sheep, then bread and cakes, then baskets, stools, and chairs, and finally fruits of every kind. So many people had crowded into the cave that by the time Tiny John got there he couldn't see a thing. So little by little he squeezed and worked his way up to the manger.

What a beautiful sight he saw. Joseph and Mary were sitting there, calm and peaceful. He was startled at the sight of the three kings dressed in their exquisite robes. Then there were the shepherds and the many varied gifts they brought. For just a fleeting moment Tiny John remembered sadly that he had no gift for the king. The infant king! Why, he was so excited that he had almost forgotten about the baby. He stood up on his toes and looked into the crib.

What a beautiful sight he beheld. There was the new baby laying in the straw. He was so clean and shiny, bright and pink in his nakedness that Tiny John had to rub his eyes to focus them. When they did, his body warmed lovingly to the sight they beheld. Oh, how he loved babies! Perhaps it was because they were small like him. Whatever the reason, his heart went out to them—all of them.

He stared in wonder at the baby's tiny face. He looked lovingly at his little nose and tiny ears. The baby's hands were ever so small and clenched so tightly. His tummy was smooth and shiny. His little legs curled up in front of him as if he were trying to make himself into a ball. Tiny John gazed in wonder at his knees and feet and little toes. He stood there poised at the tips of his toes, holding onto the side of the manger for support. He could hear the others whispering around him, "What a beautiful baby." "Look at how richly the kings are dressed." "See the nice gifts the child got." And in a slightly more subdued voice some peasants were bickering over who had brought the better gifts. Amid all this whispering Tiny John gazed in rapt attention at the infant before him.

At last it began to impress itself upon him that something was wrong. He stretched higher so that he could see better. Something was wrong with the baby. But what? What could be wrong? He looked closer, more critically. What could it be? The baby had curled himself almost into a ball. Then he noticed it. He was shivering. The baby was shivering from the cold. He was cuddling up to get body heat the way Tiny John did in his own bed on cold nights. The baby was cold, for he had no clothes to warm him. The night air outside was cold, and it was even colder in the cave.

Tiny John stepped down, hoping to tell Joseph and Mary about the baby. There were so many people standing around the manger that they couldn't see the child. They couldn't see that he was shivering from the cold. Tiny John tried to force his way to them but there were too many people in the way. He tried pushing past them but they quickly put him in his place. There was nothing he could do short of shouting, which he knew would only bring remonstrations. He looked about helplessly. Before him on the earthen floor were the

153

gifts that had been presented to the child. He searched among them for something he could put over the baby to warm him. There were so many things—pots, pans, cakes, food, baskets, even gold, frankincense and myhrr. But there were no clothes, no blankets.

Tiny John tried to tell the shepherds, but the moment he spoke they warned him to be quiet or leave the stable. It was useless. No one would listen to him.

It was then, as always, in the midst of his utter helplessness that the idea came to him. He struggled through the crowd back to the crib. Standing before the manger he lifted off his tunic. Holding his garment in his hands, he now stood naked before the babe and assemblage. The cold air chilled his unprotected body. "No matter," he thought. "I can take the cold better than the child because I'm older even if I'm not much bigger." He stood on his tiptoes, reached over the rim of the manger and placed his tunic over the baby.

It was this gesture that drew the attention of the townspeople. There was an audible gasp when they saw what Tiny John had done.

"Get that dirty tunic off the baby!" someone shouted. Then another chimed in: "How dare he put that dirty robe on the king!" The chorus began to swell now. "Disgraceful!" "Shameful!" "Look at him standing there naked. He ought to be ashamed of himself." The crowd was becoming angry and would soon lose control.

Tiny John's father grabbed hold of him and started to carry him out of the cave as the crowd shouted: "You should punish him for putting that dirty tunic on our king."

In the midst of the angry din, as the shepherd reached the door of the stable, a gentle voice somehow stayed the rising tide. "Stop! Please stop!" As if arrested by some unseen hand, all motion, all conversation, suddenly ceased. The magi and the shepherds turned to the gentle woman. It was the babe's mother who spoke. "Bring the boy here," she said.

The shepherd turned, Tiny John still tucked under his massive arm. Slowly he walked back to the manger and released his naked son.

Tiny John stood before the gathering, feeling ever so small and so very cold. But even more distressing was his embarrassment at having everyone stare at him. No one knew what to say or how to act.

The woman looked at the kings and then at the shepherds. "Today," she said, "the Lord our God has been very good to us. Today he has given to us his Son to be our king. And by his decree, so that the whole world should know, he has summoned to his Son's throne room both the mighty and the lowly. Hence have you come to do him homage and to bring him your gifts. You have brought him gold, frankincense, and myrrh. You have brought him your sheep and baskets and fruit. There are so many wonderful gifts—gifts all fit for a king. But as you see, our God has willed for his Son to be born poor. Thus he was born here in this cold stable with naught to warm him but the breath of animals.

"And of all of you gathered here, lo, it was this tiny shepherd boy who would see his plight. The babe shivered from the cold. And because he had nothing to give, he gave all that he had—his tunic. He would go naked so that the infant king would have something to wear."

For a moment the woman stopped speaking in order to let the full impact of what she had said sink into

155

the minds and hearts of her listeners. No one spoke or moved. Then in a most solemn tone the goodly mother announced: "Tiny John showed God the greatest love of all." With that she reached down and put the shepherd boy's tunic on the baby. She then bent over and kissed Tiny John. "Thank you, John," she whispered. "Jesus will never forget your gift, I promise you."

Tiny John was so proud and happy that he was suddenly warm all over. Joseph gave his father a piece of gold and told him to buy John a new tunic. The shepherd lifted his son onto his shoulders for all to see. The three kings applauded and the shepherds cheered. Even the animals joined the accolades. The cow mooed, the donkey brayed, and the sheep bleated excitedly.

That was the first Christmas, nearly two thousand years ago. But that is not the end of the story. Legend has it that as the baby Jesus grew, the tunic that Tiny John had given him grew up with him. Jesus wore the tunic right up to the day he died. And to show just how much God loved that gift, he would not let the Roman soldiers tear it apart. Instead they cast lots for it—but it remained in one piece.

And what happened to Tiny John? The legend also states that he seemed never to grow older, passing two or three years as one. Later on he met Jesus again and became one of his closest followers. Tiny John once had given Jesus all that he had—his tunic—when Jesus was born. And when Jesus was dying on the cross, he returned the favor by giving John all that he had left—his mother.

Appendix

A Speck of Dust

Every person who prays to God has a rather specific conclusion in mind; get me this job, let me pass that exam, cure some illness. How often it seems that just when that hope is about to be fulfilled a caprice of fate changes everything. The best prayer, the ultimate prayer is abandonment, complete trust in God. Like Speck, when we finally get our wish we discover that God has something better in mind all along.

Parable of the Baker

Although this was specifically used with reference to certain U.S. foreign policy, the parable deliberately offers no solution as it can be applied to many more personal situations.

The Search

The tale represents man's personal quest for God. It incorporates such biblical themes as "unless you become as children. . . ," "God has chosen the simple to confound the wise," and the theological notion of the "leap of faith." When one has been deeply touched by God, when one has abandoned self to God in the leap of faith, when one accepts the gift freely given (not attainable by human means), or when "one has been saved," then the realization comes that what was experienced before wasn't quite the real thing.

The Encounter

This story is a classical tale of love and marriage. It was written on the occasion of my having made a marriage encounter weekend. Everything and everyone in this tale is a symbol—some of it obvious, some of it difficult. Encounter encourages dialogue, so to aid in that objective, the following symbols are listed:

Garden of Eden	world
God	deadly sins
Satan	death
Man	resurrection
Woman	
Man united with God (real marriage)	

For those familiar with the Encounter weekend, the following are also symbolized:

90–90

3-fold growth—Understanding, Acceptance, Unity (separately symbolized)

The King's New Tunic and The Juggler

These are my heart-felt gifts to the pro-life movement.

Special Angels

This story is affectionately dedicated to my beloved dog Hans. He was truly a special angel sent to me from heaven twelve years ago. He filled my life and the lives of the retarded people whom I serve and all those who had the good fortune to know him with all the qualities enumerated in my story. But most especially with love He now waits for me in heaven.

In retelling this story, the reader might add or subtract such qualities that would make the tale more personal.